"Remember when I told you that pine needles make a great bed?"

Sean lowered her to the ground, cradling her head between his hands. Andi's eyes were dark with need, her lips parted, soft and waiting. She was all he desired and more.

"How can you say we don't know each other, Andi? I know the best of you, all the secret wonderful parts of you. I know the little mole above your breast...." He kissed the spot tenderly. "I know the sounds you make when you sleep, the way you look waking up, how your face glows when we make love. I know the secret smile on your lips when I'm inside you. No one else knows that smile, Andi. No one."

His words washed over her like soft, sweet music. She felt as if her heart would burst with love as he touched her, stroked her, held her close. She gazed up at him with tears in her eyes.

"I know the best part of you, Andi. I know your heart."

The writing team of Shannon Harper and Madeline Porter—writing under the name **Madeline Harper**—love to blend laughter with romance. So when looking for new ideas, they decided to put a humorous twist on a subject as American as apple pie—tests. After all, there are driving tests, typing tests and even math tests (ugh!). Shouldn't there be a test for one of the most important decisions in life—marriage? Be sure to watch for their next book, *The Highwayman,* the exciting conclusion to Temptation's Rogues miniseries, available in September 1996.

Books by Madeline Harper

HARLEQUIN TEMPTATION
447—WEDDING BELL BLUES
476—THE PIRATE'S WOMAN
499—CHRISTMAS IN JULY
527—THE TROUBLE WITH BABIES
554—STRANGER IN MY ARMS

THE MARRIAGE TEST
MADELINE HARPER

Harlequin Books

TORONTO • NEW YORK • LONDON
AMSTERDAM • PARIS • SYDNEY • HAMBURG
STOCKHOLM • ATHENS • TOKYO • MILAN
MADRID • WARSAW • BUDAPEST • AUCKLAND

For Ann, Anne and Alice, who love Maine, too.

ISBN 0-373-25689-2

THE MARRIAGE TEST

Copyright © 1996 by Madeline Porter & Shannon Harper.

Prologue

Saint Moritz, Switzerland

HE SLID his hands along her body, sensuously caressing her damp, warm skin. She closed her eyes and gave herself to his touch. Hot and heady, it warmed her thoroughly, causing a tremor to travel along her skin—from the tender softness of her earlobe to the hollow between her breasts to the inner flesh of her thighs. A smile curved her lips.

She pushed his hair away from his forehead and then kissed his face, tasting his salty sweetness with her tongue. "Love in the afternoon," she said, "in front of a blazing fire. Then dinner in bed . . ." She paused, frowning. "Don't we have that backward?"

"Hmm?" he asked lazily.

"It's supposed to be dinner in front of the fire and *then* lovemaking in bed."

"This works for me," he said.

Their clothes were scattered across the floor, and empty dishes were stacked haphazardly on the room service cart.

She sighed deeply. "Sometimes I think I'm dreaming."

"Oh, babe, it doesn't get any more real than this." He turned, covering her body with his, and they made hot, greedy love as the blazing fire dwindled to glowing embers.

HOURS LATER, propped against eiderdown pillows, they shared a goblet of champagne in their rumpled king-size bed.

"Isn't reality wonderful?" she asked with a giggle.

He put the glass on the bedside table and settled against the pillows, his hands folded behind his head. His broad chest with its dusting of golden hair gleamed in the soft light of the bedside lamp. She wondered if he knew how well the provocative pose showed off the delineation of muscles in his arms and shoulders. Or how perfectly the lamplight cast shadows in just the right places along the strong planes of his face and the sensuous curve of his mouth.

Sean Fleming was used to posing. Most of the time it was in front of cameras, but he'd probably had opportunities in other places, as well, including the bedroom. One of his greatest appeals was his absolute assurance. Like everything else about him, that turned her on.

He was World Wide Network's number-one foreign correspondent; power and success were his. He was tall, muscular and dangerously good-looking, and at thirty-two there was something untamed about him. Maybe it was his tawny hair, worn a little long, or the all-knowing gaze in his gray eyes.

The miracle was that he seemed as crazy over her as she was about him.

She'd seen him the first night of her vacation in the hotel's après-ski bar. He was surrounded by a host of what she called Euro-ski bunnies, gorgeous women with perfect figures in stunning clothes. He looked up, just as in a romantic movie, and met her eyes across the room. He smiled; she returned the smile. And he made his way to her.

She knew who he was, of course. Everyone knew Sean Fleming, award-winning journalist, who covered the news around the globe. She'd seen him often on television, standing in a bombed-out building, reporting calmly and coolly in his crisp khakis while explosions surrounded him. Who wouldn't have fallen in love with him?

They had drinks together that first night, followed by dinner and dancing. Then they went to her room. She didn't hesitate, didn't take time to think. This was *it*. Nothing like this had ever happened to her, and she knew it never would again.

Their lovemaking had been like spontaneous combustion, and for two weeks they'd barely been apart.

SEAN SHIFTED in the bed and pulled Andi closer. What a vacation this had turned out to be! Just when he'd begun to get bored with the usual crowd, he'd spotted Andrea Kent. Since that evening, she'd filled a void in his life he hadn't even realized was there.

"More champagne, babe?" He reached for the almost-empty bottle.

"Nope. My head's fuzzy enough. I don't want to forget these last hours before I leave. Every minute with you is too important."

His heart gave an unexpected lurch. Andi was the most honest woman he'd ever met. No games. No subterfuge. She was bright, warm and spontaneous, and her brown eyes looked at the world and saw it as it was.

He liked everything about her, especially the incredible sex appeal she exuded. Just thinking of Andi excited him and made him want her with a heavy, throbbing ache. He'd never had such a visceral response to any woman.

And he wasn't about to let her go.

"I love you, Andi," he blurted before he had time to think. Well, what the hell. He had to say something, and dammit, it was true. He did love her.

"And I love you, Sean," she replied in a tremulous voice. "I've never felt this way before."

He took her into his arms, and a long shudder of desire rippled down his spine. He wanted her—again, so soon and so intensely that it made his head spin. How could it be possible for her to consume him this completely?

As the blood pounded wildly in his veins, he heard himself tell her, "You're not leaving, Andi."

"Sean, I—"

"No," he whispered against her lips. "Don't say anything more." He kissed her hungrily, unable to think of anything but Andi and making love to her for the rest of his life. "We're going to be together. We're getting married."

ANDI WOKE FIRST, pulled on her robe and went to the window. Looming before her were the snow-covered

Alps, which had drawn her on this spur-of-the-moment vacation, one of the few impulsive moves in a life that was usually much more deliberate. What followed in the next two weeks had been one spontaneous decision after another, including the one that would affect her forever—to marry Sean.

And it was so right. Theirs was the kind of romance every woman dreamed of, and Sean was the kind of man every woman wanted. She was going to grab for happiness with both hands and never let go.

She hugged herself tightly. They'd agreed to marry as soon as possible, and that made her giddy with happiness. Now they'd never have to say goodbye. Since he was the network's fair-haired boy, he would have his pick of any post and could choose New York or Washington, D.C. or maybe Los Angeles. She would be happy in any of those places.

She wasn't really thinking of a house in the suburbs with a white picket fence, but why not? Once they were married, their lives would change. She expected compromise—on both their parts. It would help them build a life together.

They were a perfect couple!

Sean opened his eyes and saw her standing at the window, framed in the moonlight. His wife-to-be. Funny, but the words didn't scare him at all. In fact, the thought of marrying Andi gave him a deep sense of satisfaction.

She was perfect for him. Spontaneous but level-headed. Hardworking. Independent. Beautiful. Sexy as hell. And very capable of taking care of herself when he was away.

Of course, when he got back from wherever the network sent him, she'd be waiting. Then there'd be an earthshaking, fireworks-making homecoming. That thought was enough to propel him out of bed.

Naked, he stood behind her at the window, putting his arms around her with a deep, satisfied sigh. "Come back to bed, Andi. I want to celebrate our last sinful night together as unmarried lovers—"

She pressed against his warmth. "Before our sinless years together as old married folks?"

"Married, even old, someday. But always sinful." Sean grinned and led her to the bed. This marriage was made in heaven.

1

Clarion, Maine
Eighteen months later

ANDREA KENT FLEMING struggled out of bed and reached for her robe, which she dragged behind her as she stumbled through the bedroom door to the second-floor landing in her father's house. Leaning against the rail, she muttered, "Who could be ringing the doorbell at—" She pushed a clump of tangled hair from her face and checked the grandfather clock at the top of the stairs. "At five in the morning?"

By the time she'd reached the first floor and crossed the foyer, she'd managed to get her robe over one arm and as far as her shoulder. She stopped there and peered through the peephole. And suddenly she was wide awake. The robe fell to the floor as she pulled open the front door.

"Do you have any idea what time it is?" was all she could manage to utter as her husband stepped inside.

"That's not very welcoming from my loving wife."

"It's a lot more welcoming than the rude question I was tempted to ask."

He dropped his canvas bag with a thud on the hardwood floor. "Which was?"

Facing him in nothing but her shortie nightgown, Andi tried to keep her cool. "Why didn't you let me know you were coming?"

"I was expecting a rude quesion."

"All right, then. How about, what the hell are you doing here?"

He laughed. "That's more like it. The answer is, I wanted to surprise you."

"No, you didn't. You wanted to throw me off balance, and you succeeded. You should have called first, Sean."

"If I'd done that, you would have told me to stay away. I thought we needed to talk face-to-face."

"And *I* thought the telephone was sufficient for handling our business."

"Sufficient?" Sean repeated in amazement. "I fly halfway across the world, land in New York late at night, go to my office and find divorce papers waiting for me—and you think a couple of phone conversations are *sufficient?*"

"We've used the phone for the past six months," she reminded him. "Ever since I came home from Europe. Ever since my father died. You knew exactly how I felt. We've talked and talked and talked. And before that, I told you loud and clear when I left Casablanca—"

"It was Tangier."

"Excuse me," she replied sarcastically, "but after a while, one city begins to look just like another. As for the damned hotel rooms, they looked alike from the beginning."

Sean started to challenge that, changed his mind and asked, "Are we going to stand in the hall arguing or are you going to offer me a drink?"

"At five in the morning?" she asked with astonishment.

"My need for a drink is dictated by circumstances, not by the time of day," he answered.

Andi's lips tightened. "Go into the den. There's brandy on the bookcase. I'm going to get dressed."

Sean's lips curved in the slow, provocative smile she remembered so well, the smile she'd never been able to resist. Until now.

"I like the way you look. Little short see-through nightie—"

"That's exactly why I'm changing." She'd already managed to scoop up her robe and put it on. She wrapped the sash around her waist, turned and fled up the stairs with his voice trailing behind her.

"'Course, I like you better in nothing at all. I'm trying to imagine how you'd look, running up the stairs in the buff—"

She made it to her bedroom, slammed the door behind her and let out a low curse. She didn't like the way things were going; she didn't like it one damned bit. She had told him on the phone that talking wasn't going to save their marriage.

In fact, she didn't want it saved. She wanted out. No alimony. No division of communal property—not that there was any to divide. Just whatever had been in the suitcases they'd dragged from one hotel room to the next. All she wanted was a simple, civilized, unemotional divorce ending a marriage that never should have been.

Saying all that on the phone and putting it in legal papers was one thing; facing him with it was another. That's why she'd admonished him to stay away. But here he was, living proof that seeing Sean and keeping her emotions in check were mutually exclusive.

Like now. Her hands were shaking, and she couldn't seem to get her breathing under control. He'd always stirred up powerful emotions in her. At first it had been unabashed passion. Now it was anger, bright and burning. In order to keep the passion at bay, she needed to hold onto the anger, clamping onto it with both hands. It was her only protection from Sean's charm and charisma.

It hadn't worked that well when she opened the door and saw him for the first time in months. But she'd been thrown off balance by the sight of him. Even at five in the morning, he looked fabulous, with his tousled hair, the faint trace of whiskers and gray eyes that were softly, sexily sleepy.

She'd always found the perfect words to describe him—from the very beginning—words like masculine, exciting, charismatic, compelling. Those words and more had popped into her head when she'd seen him standing in the doorway. It wouldn't happen again. He'd caught her off guard, but from now on, she would be prepared. "And strong," she advised aloud. "Be prepared and strong, and you won't get involved again."

She shimmied out of her gown, pulled on a T-shirt and reached for a pair of jeans. Taking them from the hanger, she paused and thought about her advice to herself. Knowing better was one thing. Acting on that knowledge was another. She admonished herself firmly. "If you don't watch out, you'll find yourself in a hell of a mess."

She pulled on the jeans, zipped them up and looked at herself in the mirror. It was necessary to at least brush her hair, which she did quickly, but not to put on makeup or do anything that might cause Sean to look twice—or comment. In fact, she decided, taking off the T-shirt and putting on an oversize blouse, shapeless was the best choice.

SEAN POURED HIMSELF a brandy. So what if it wasn't yet dawn? Still suffering from jet lag, he'd gotten into a car and driven for eight hours to get here, so who knew what time it was on his biological clock? He took a big swig, savoring the good brandy. What the hell? It was cocktail time plenty of places in the world.

Drink in hand, he settled into a worn leather chair, put his feet on the ottoman and took a look around the room where he'd been banished. It was dominated by a huge fireplace, flanked by two overstuffed sofas. Bookcases were filled with well-worn volumes, and more books were stacked on a corner desk. The colors in the Oriental carpet were softly faded. It was a room that beckoned and welcomed, a room that stated *home* loud and clear.

After a while, he got up and walked to the fireplace for a better look at a familiar photograph, the family picture that had been displayed in every hotel room they'd shared during their six months together abroad. Andi, her sister, Pam, their mother, who had died years before, and their father. It was his death that had brought Andi home.

Now, only the sisters were left. Andi looked solemnly into the camera, her arm protectively around Pam. He put the photo carefully on the mantel.

It was going to be tough, Sean realized, the battle to get back his wife. She was determined to win. But he had his own agenda. "I'm not going to make it easy for you, babe," he said softly.

When she came into the room, she seemed a little out of breath. Her curly brown hair was brushed from her face, which was pink and glowing. He noticed immediately that she wasn't wearing makeup. It had a wonderful effect on him. He liked the fresh and wholesome look. It reminded him of the woman he'd fallen in love with. Except *that* Andi had been open and inviting, her eyes bright with curiosity, her smile warm and welcoming. This Andi was suspicious and distant, treating him as if he was a stranger.

"I see you found the brandy."

"Very nice," he replied, taking another sip.

"My father's. He was the connoisseur of the family."

He saw her face tighten with sadness. Awkwardly, he touched her shoulder. "Listen, I'm sorry I didn't make it to the funeral, but I had to cover the economic summit, Andi. I couldn't get out of it."

She moved away and sat in the leather chair. "Of course not," she said with a degree of sarcasm. "I know how important those economic summits can be, particularly as compared to the funeral of your wife's father."

"Andi, don't—"

"But what about everything that came before, when he first got sick?"

"I was in—Zaire, I believe. Or maybe—" He couldn't actually remember.

"Wherever," she said coolly. "I'm sure it was a good story, which you certainly wouldn't have wanted to interrupt for something as trivial as my father's illness."

"For God's sake, Andi, I didn't see your dad's illness as trivial. I wanted to be with you—"

"But duty called."

He remembered. "It *was* Zaire. When you left, I was on the way there. Remember?"

She turned her head away. "So I came home alone, nursed my father for all those months—"

"I knew you had your sister to help."

"Give me a break, Sean. Pam was devastated by Dad's illness—besides being in the early stages of her pregnancy, complete with morning sickness. She was no help at all. It was up to me to take charge."

Sean dropped onto the sofa. "Which you did very well. That came across when we talked on the phone. You always sounded as if everything was in perfect control, Andi. I assumed Pam was helping, but even on your own, you could have handled things, or so I thought. You never told me—"

"I didn't think I'd have to explain my emotional state or beg my husband to come home to me." Her voice vibrated with bitterness and a touch of tears. "I thought you'd *want* to be with me."

Sean let a silent moment pass. Andi's tears disappeared, but her attitude remained. Her eyes guarded, her chin firmly set, she looked about as approachable as a cactus. But the determination not to yield to him made Sean want her more than ever.

"Is that what the divorce is about?" he asked finally in a quiet voice. "Because I didn't come back for the funeral?"

She gave him a pitying look. "That remark shows how little you know me."

"Then what—"

"The divorce is about our marriage, Sean—or lack of it."

He held up his left hand and displayed his wedding ring. "I've been faithful to you, Andi. I wear this ring because I'm married, *we're* married. We took vows, we lived together."

"No, we didn't!" Andi jumped to her feet and turned toward him accusingly. "We had a series of one-night stands. I was in Rome while you were in Bosnia. You flew in for a weekend. We made love, drank wine, and then you were off again. Next I was in Barcelona, waiting until you returned from Syria—"

"Some people would consider that the perfect marriage," he commented.

"Well, I'm not some people. Being left in a hotel room for weeks at a time isn't my idea of a relationship, much less a marriage."

"You weren't left in a hotel room, for God's sake, Andi. You traveled to some of the world's most fascinating cities. You were an independent and intelligent woman with the opportunity to explore Istanbul, Madrid, Stockholm—"

"The tourist bit gets to be a drag after a while. Especially when you have no friends, no job—and no work permit to get one—not to mention the language barrier. The network didn't supply me bilingual gofers and assistants," she added pointedly. "After a while, all I could do was wait for my husband to drop in on me. That's not exactly what I expected."

"So what did you expect?" he challenged.

"A life together, a place to call our own and a job for me, too—maybe even one that was fulfilling and interesting. I hadn't counted on living in half the hotel rooms in Europe. I missed having a...a home." She said it almost defensively.

Sean glanced around the room. "Something like this, I suppose, reeking with stability? With worn leather and family photos? You know I'm not a traditional kind of person, Andi."

She met his eyes squarely. "I didn't know I was, either, until I started living like a Gypsy. I can't do it, Sean."

"Marriage is a compromise," he countered.

Andi let out a frustrated sigh. "Who compromised?" She didn't wait for his answer. "I did. I was thousands of miles from my family and friends, I gave up my career and my home. Nothing changed in your life. Oh, I take that back," she added sarcastically. "When you got married, you got a regular bed partner who would be waiting for you," she accused angrily.

"Just a minute, Andi." She looked like she was about to spring at him, eyes blazing, fists clenched at her sides. "We can talk about all this, but only if you calm down."

"I don't want to calm down. And I don't want to talk about this. What I want is for you to leave."

Sean didn't budge from the sofa. Instead, he put down his glass and said quietly, "I'm not going to leave. So you might as well get used to that, babe. I'm going to stay here as long as it takes to save this marriage. I've listened to everything you've said, believe it or not. And I understand. Maybe I didn't compromise before, but now I'm willing to."

She narrowed her eyes suspiciously. "Like—how?"

"I've been offered a new job by the network. Bureau chief in London." He waited for her reaction. It didn't come. "London! Think of it, Andi. We'll be able to live in a great city, where everyone speaks English, where we can have a house and garden, afternoons in the park, theater and concerts. We can have whatever you want." He grinned cockily. "A normal life, babe."

"You don't have a clue about a normal life. Have fun in London. I have plans of my own."

She sank into the chair and put her feet on the ottoman. It was wickedly pleasurable to watch the surprise, then disappointment register on Sean's face. Obviously, he thought she was so easy that she'd fall into his arms at the mere promise of a life-style change. Maybe she would have—if she didn't know better, if she didn't know that after a month in London, he'd get restless. Then bored. Then he'd be on the road again, leaving her where she was before, caught in a one-person marriage.

"What kind of plans?" he asked.

"Personal and professional," she answered enigmatically. Again, she enjoyed watching his expression change, this time to curiosity.

"So you're forcing me to ask. What are you talking about?"

One by one she ticked the items off her fingers. "First, Pam has finally agreed to sell Kent Unlimited. Second, once the store is sold, she and Kevin will move into this house. Third, I'll be out of here, no longer tied down—free. I'm going to work for TSS in New York."

"Okay, I give up. What's TSS?"

"Television Shopping Service," she said triumphantly.

Sean burst into laughter. "You've got to be kidding! Isn't that the network devoted entirely to conspicuous consumption? Viewers call in and buy stuff hawked by curvy women. Don't tell me you're going to sell fake diamond necklaces on television."

She was livid. "What a put-down remark."

"I'm sorry, Andi—"

"Your apology is *not* accepted," she replied. "I can't believe your attitude. Just because you're a big-deal television reporter, you don't think anything else matters. Well, let me tell you, Sean Fleming, television shopping is a multibillion-dollar industry, and

Michael has offered me an excellent job in the TSS marketing department."

"Michael?"

"Michael Rossi, the CEO. I met him though Kent Unlimited." She lifted her chin defensively, daring him to make another smart remark.

For a while he didn't say anything. Then he asked, "Does this Michael have something to do with your divorce plans?"

"You *would* think that. Sorry to disappoint you, Sean, but another man is not high on my wish list right now. If it wasn't for your vanity, you'd get that. Michael is a good friend who has been very supportive."

"Unlike your husband."

"You said it." She stood up. "This is my time, Sean. My father's pain and suffering are over. Pam's sadness has dissipated, and she's devoting herself to her husband and the baby they're expecting. The store's going up for sale. I'm on my own. With only three things to worry about—*my* needs, *my* career, *my* life."

He'd watched her spring from the chair and pace back and forth as she talked. "That was quite a speech, Andi. Now is it my turn?"

"I'm going to make some coffee," she said, ignoring his question, "so you won't fall asleep driving back to New York."

She started toward the door. It was almost over. She didn't need to listen to his side of the story. Instead, she'd make sure he left as soon as he'd had some coffee. Just a few more minutes of holding herself together, and then she'd be free of the memories, free of wanting him, free from wishing for what might have been.

Just as she reached the door, he surged from his seat, crossed the room in three long strides and grasped her arm. "I said I wanted my turn."

"Sorry. You don't get a turn." She tried to pull away, but he held her tightly.

"I'm not giving up. You know me better than that. I want a second chance, and I'm damned well going to have it."

"Sean, please. I don't want a scene."

"Neither do I, but you're going to listen."

"I've heard all I need to hear." She struggled against him, pushing at his chest, trying to move out of the circle of his arms, trying not to be affected by his closeness. But a wave of potent memories had already washed over her. She remembered the excitement of his hands, not roughly holding her arms as she struggled but sweetly caressing her skin. She remembered the feeling of his lips on hers, his tongue in her mouth, the taste of him. The excitement and pleasure they gave each other, the laughter of their days, the passion of their nights, she remembered it all—in spite of herself. And the remembrance made her dizzy.

Willing herself not to think about the past, with a burst of strength, she pulled free of him. "I'm going to make coffee." She stated her plan with total determination.

Sean followed her, his heart racing. He was pretty sure she felt what he did, the rush of desire, the heat of need. Their bonds of intimacy were too powerful to sever so quickly. He felt that emphatically, deep in his heart. He wasn't going to give her up without a fight.

Andi flipped on the light in the old-fashioned kitchen. He waited in the doorway, careful not to follow her too closely and get involved in another battle. Stay cool, he told himself, leaning against the doorjamb and following her with his eyes as she moved around the kitchen.

She opened a can of coffee, measured two scoops into the filter and filled the pot with water. And all the while her hands shook. The shaking gave him a surge of promise. She could deny it if she wanted to, but Sean saw that she was as affected by their reunion as he.

He was passionately drawn to her. He couldn't seem to control his urges. He walked over and slid his arms around her waist.

She stiffened, but he didn't let her go. Her body felt wonderfully familiar and yet mysteriously tantalizing. Her hair tickled his nose, and he drew in a long breath, inhaling her scent.

Her head tilted down, her eyes avoiding him, and the gesture caused her hair to fall over her face. A portion of her neck was exposed. He longed to run his tongue along her smooth white skin. He wanted to kiss the delicious column of her neck and rediscover the taste of her. But Andi's body language was not welcoming. She was rigid, offering no sign of compromise or surrender. She refused to turn and face him.

He let her go. He could see her body relax slightly, but at least his release encouraged her to turn and look at him.

"I want a chance, Andi. I think I deserve that."

She let out a shaky sigh.

He plunged headfirst into the speech he'd rehearsed during the long drive from New York City. He was able to sway millions in the television audience with the power of his words. All he wanted now was to persuade one woman of his love.

"What I'm proposing is a second honeymoon," he said. "Just you and me for two weeks, with time to talk and remember why we fell in love in the first place."

Andi glanced toward the door, looking as if she wanted to escape. Then she gathered herself together. He saw her breasts rise and fall as she breathed deeply.

"Just two weeks," he continued. "Together. You'll have a chance to see for yourself how I've changed."

She remained silent, her face expressionless.

"After that, if you still want me out of your life, I'll go quietly. No hassle. I'll sign all the papers you send my way. You'll have your divorce—and your freedom. But I'm counting on that never happening, because I know you'll feel the same as I do. You'll want me the way I want you."

The nearness of her was like a drug. He pushed aside a strand of wayward hair, still longing to kiss the hollow at her throat. Being this close to her set his blood on fire. He found himself taking the same kind of long, deep breath Andi had just struggled with.

Then she twisted away, her face flushed and her eyes bright with confusion. "Finish making the coffee," she said. "I'm going for a walk."

"I'll go with you. It's still dark—"

"The sun's just coming up, but even in the dark, it's perfectly safe here. This is Clarion, Maine, not New York City." She grabbed her jacket from a hook on the wall. "I need to think."

Then she was gone.

Sean wasn't discouraged. In fact, a satisfied smile played along his lips. He turned on the coffee maker. Yep, she was definitely confused. You might even say she was wavering. Andi would give him a chance. She was too fair and honest not to.

So they'd have their two weeks. But where? A luxury resort would be perfect. Maybe someplace in the States, since Europe wasn't presently high on her list. It would have to be far from here, though, from the store, her sister and this Michael guy.

California. A romantic hotel in Sausilito overlooking the bay. Or a rustic inn at Carmel. Or maybe the elegance of the Biltmore in Santa Barbara, the Bel Air in Los Angeles. Possibilities were endless.

There'd be room service, satin sheets, magnums of champagne, bowls of caviar. A private Jacuzzi, of course. Vases of red roses filling their suite.

Whatever it took to get her back.

2

ANDI WALKED resolutely up the hill without the slightest idea where she was going. Only when she got to the top did she realize she was heading straight for her sister's house.

Why in the world would she be going there?

Andi couldn't answer that. Of people to turn to when her life was in a mess, Pam wasn't her first choice. But Pam *was* her sister. Besides, she was there. At this hour of the morning, barging in on anyone else was unthinkable. And she sure as hell had to talk to someone. She couldn't handle this alone.

The morning breeze was cool on her flushed cheeks, but a fresh summer dawn couldn't do a thing to dampen her turmoil. Neither could the view of the harbor coming to life.

Lights from fishing and lobster boats were reflected picturesquely in the waters of Penobscot Bay as their crews got ready for the day's work. That was the charm of Clarion, and for the first eighteen years of her life, it had been enough. Then her horizons had widened. There'd been college and a series of retail jobs in Boston. She'd been promoted to buyer for an upscale department store and found a wonderful, sunny apartment that she adored. Then she'd taken that impulsive ski trip to Europe and met Sean.

Even though she'd outgrown Clarion, her family's New England blood still ran richly in her veins, a heritage she could never completely outgrow. She believed in hard work and craved a place of her own, not her father's house, but certainly not a series of hotel rooms, either. Sean was right. She was more traditional than she'd ever imagined.

As she approached Pam's house, she noticed with relief that a light was on in the kitchen. She climbed the steps and knocked softly on the door.

Pam appeared, wearing a robe and a sleepy look. "Andi, it's not even six in the morning. What're you doing up?"

"I was going to ask you the same thing," Andi responded. "What a surprise to see a light on. I'd expected to camp out on the steps until the household came to life."

"Half the household's already gone. Kevin bid on a remodeling job in Rockland—and got it. A great job but too far away."

"You take what you get in construction, Pam."

"Yeah, even if it means I barely get to see him for the next month. But the money'll help. Thank heaven summer's here—construction season. I just hope the next job is closer to home." Pam held up the coffeepot. "Want some?"

"Sure." Andi sat down at the table in the kitchen, which was small and cramped like the rest of the house Pam and Kevin were anxious to leave. Following up on that thought, she made an offer. "I know you and Kevin want to get settled, especially with the baby on the way. Why don't you go ahead and move into Dad's house with me before I leave?"

"There's still time," Pam said, patting her very round stomach. "Besides..." She hesitated while pouring the coffee and then easing into a chair beside her sister. "I have some mixed feelings, Andi."

"You don't want to move into the house?"

"Of course, I do. And so does Kevin. It'll be perfect for us. But, well, I wish you wouldn't leave. And if we sell the store, you will."

"Pam, we've been through all this. Clarion is great for you—"

"I know, but you're more ambitious. You always have been."

"My future isn't here. That's one thing I'm certain of. But you can't manage the store alone, not with the baby coming. We *have* to sell. The decision's been made. It's over. Done."

Pam pursed her lips, putting on the petulant look that she'd worn off and on since childhood, an expression Andi knew only too well. "I just want things to stay the same."

"They won't. They can't. Life's not like that." Andi smiled ruefully. "It's more complicated. And when you think you have everything figured out, your whole world goes crazy."

Pam put down her coffee cup and looked directly at her sister. The pout had disappeared, and she bit quizzically at her lip. "Something's going on," she said finally. "You didn't come knocking at the door before sunrise for no reason. What's the matter?"

"Not what. Who. Sean's in town."

Pam gave a little shriek. "Sean? Your Sean?"

"My Sean. He's at the house now, drinking coffee and waiting for me to consider a reconciliation."

"You're not going to, are you? I thought he was out of your life for good."

"I thought so, too, but..." Andi pushed away from the table, stood and began what passed for pacing in the limited space. "I was sure it was over, that I could get a divorce and move on. But when I saw him, when he touched me, something happened."

"Shivers," Pam said with a lift of her dark eyebrows.

"You've got that right." She shivered involuntarily, just remembering his kiss on her neck.

"Raging hormones," Pam added.

"Mmm. That, plus memories of the good times."

"What about the bad ones?"

"I remember those, too. He says he's changed, but how can I be sure? He wants another chance, but how can I trust him? Dammit, Pam, what am I going to do?"

"I can't believe you're asking me. I'm usually the one who wants advice, not the one who gives it."

Andi suddenly stopped pacing and sat down, finally understanding why she had come here. "But when it comes to things like this, relationships, what goes on between men and women—"

Pam patted her stomach again. "I know a few things about that," she said with a laugh.

Andi grasped her sister's hands. "Then tell me what to do. I need help, Pam."

Pam narrowed her brown eyes thoughtfully. "My gut opinion is that you should tell him to get out of town. Leave. Go away. Scram. Vamoose."

"I get the idea," Andi said dryly.

"He took you away from the family, and he made your life miserable."

Andi sighed loudly.

Pam echoed the sigh. "But I know you won't do that. So I guess you'll have to give him a second chance. If you don't—"

"If I don't, I'll never be really sure. I'll always wonder."

Pam hoisted herself from the chair and took a bowl from the cabinet. "Cereal? I'm hungry all the time."

"No, thanks. I need to get home and work this out with Sean. You've been a great help, Sis."

"I didn't help," Pam said. "I only confirmed what you'd already decided." Her lips began a pout. "I guess you'll be zooming off to some romantic spot—"

"We haven't discussed it. I realize it's a bad time to leave Clarion, with the sale of the store still pending—not to mention my new nephew or niece. But we'll work something out."

Pam's face brightened. "Why not stay here? Try having a second honeymoon in Clarion and see what the glamorous Sean Fleming is like around real people."

"Sean in Clarion? No way." The idea was ridiculous . . . but intriguing.

"Why not?" Pam persisted. "You could try living in a house instead of a hotel, facing the normal problems of married life—the kind Kevin and I deal with every day."

A smile lit Andi's face. "I love the way you're thinking. If we lived like real people, that would mean taking out the garbage, mowing the lawn, shopping at the local market—like a married couple!"

"I wonder if he could take it?"

Andi laughed. "Are you kidding? He'd hire a full staff of servants within a day. Nope, whether we go to a luxury hotel or stay right here, Sean won't be able to shake the whole life-style of the rich and famous thing."

Pam was thoughtful for a moment. "What if..."

Andi looked at her sister curiously.

"I hate to suggest you leave Clarion, but Pawlie's Island isn't that far away. What if you went over there, to the cabin?"

Andi couldn't contain her excitement. "You're filled with great ideas, Pam. Pawlie's Island! It's close enough to Clarion so I can rush home if you need me, but it's isolated enough that we'd have to depend on each other. There wouldn't be another living soul around."

"It sounds pretty scary."

Andi's heart pounded rapidly. "It is scary. And exciting. It's just the test we need."

"Will he agree?"

"If he's serious about giving our marriage a second try, he will." Andi gave Pam a quick hug.

"But will he *pass*?"

"You don't think so, huh?"

"You said it, not me," Pam replied. "But if past performance is any indication . . . well, he didn't do so good at the real thing."

"And I shouldn't expect him to improve, but who knows—maybe he will, now that he realizes I'm serious—and if he really wants us to get back together. It's worth a try."

"And this will decide things once and for all?"

"Yes. I promise. If he doesn't pass this test, it's all over, and I go on with my life. But if he does—well, I'm not going to think that far ahead."

"No reason to."

"There you go again, insinuating that he won't pass."

"Maybe I am, but the prediction is based on what you've told me about him, Andi."

"So be blunt. What do you really think?"

Pam crossed her arms over her ample belly. "Chances are slim to none that he'll conform. Sorry, Andi. That's my gut feeling. Now tell me what you think."

"Me? I have no idea. But I guess I'm going to find out."

"YOU'VE GOT TO BE KIDDING! A marriage test? No way." Sean's gray eyes darkened with disbelief. He'd left the kitchen and was sitting on the back steps, warming in the morning sun.

"You're the one who wanted a second honeymoon." Andi stripped off her jacket and leaned against the railing, her arms folded across her chest.

"A honeymoon, not a test. I want us to be together as man and wife, not as student and teacher, for God's sake, Andi."

She shrugged.

"Come on, babe, be serious."

"I've never been more serious in my life."

"All right." He backed off a little. "Suppose I agree to this test. Why does it have to be here? In Maine?"

"Maine's a wonderful place," she said stubbornly. "You act as if it's Antarctica."

Sean ran his hands through his thick hair, as millions of Americans had seen him do so often on television. The gesture was calculated to show seriousness, contemplation. The TV public might be taken-in by the gesture. It didn't faze her.

"I'm sure Maine is great, but I had other places in mind—"

"Your way or no way, huh? Sounds familiar."

He considered. "What's your idea?"

"Our family has a cabin on a coastal island. We could go there."

She saw him brighten. Of course he would! Sean did damned well on islands. Mykonos. Ibiza. Antigua. Sunlit days, moonlit nights.

"Sounds interesting," he admitted.

"Fine. The place is decided. Now there's the test."

Sean shrugged. "How difficult can it be?"

"Here's how difficult. I want us to act like a real married couple—"

Sean cocked his eyebrow. "Now, that part I like." He ran his hand under her sleeve and up her bare arm. "I've missed you, Andi."

She moved her arm out of his reach and held her hand up. "I don't mean sleeping together, Sean. I mean a lot more."

"Sure, I know that." He nodded reflexively while he allowed his busy mind to undress her.

First that damned oversize shirt, which she'd worn for a reason—without counting on his imagination. He'd be willing to bet she wasn't wearing a bra. Then the jeans. He could peel them off easily. They'd made love many places but never on the back porch of an old frame house in coastal Maine.

He dragged his mind to Andi's explanation.

"We've always lived in hotels with room service and maid service and every other kind of service you can name," she reminded him. "We've never shared the ordinary ebb and flow of married life. Everything about our time together has been so . . . artificial."

"Not true, Andi." He stretched his long legs and looked at her. "Why don't you sit down?"

She shook her head.

"Then I'll stand up." He started to rise, but she held out her hand.

"Let's just stay like this."

"All right, I'll agree, but I can't agree with what you said about our lives together, Andi. Some things were very real." He let the seductive drawl creep into his voice. "Remember?"

Her eyes met his then flicked away as she went on, determinedly, with her spiel. "I'm talking about everyday life, Sean. We've never known that. We were either together in fantasyland—or thousands of miles apart."

"Aching for each other," he added. "And when we got together, it was great, wasn't it?"

She shrugged. "Whether it was or not, it wasn't real. I want us to try living together as husband and wife with no drama, no glamour—and no separations. That's real life. Real marriage."

"You're talking about playing house, taking out the garbage, doing the dishes. That's no more married life than a weekend at the Gritti in Venice. They're both *part* of what it's all about."

"Exactly," she agreed. "And what it's all about is spending time together. The island is isolated so we'll be dependent on each other and no one else. Like a pioneer family in a way."

That sounded better. He and Andi alone with plenty of time and privacy. How bad could it be? He smiled at her. "Sounds great."

"Don't accept too quickly, Sean. Remember that there's no room service. We have to take care of ourselves."

Sean shrugged. "For how long?"

"Um, about two weeks. I can't be away any longer than that because of Pam's baby. I want to be around when it's born."

"Two weeks," he echoed, pretending serious consideration. Inside he was chortling. Two weeks? Nothing to it. He could do anything for two weeks, certainly take out the trash. After that, he and Andi would be together again for good. He'd pass her damned marriage test with flying colors. "I think I can handle it."

"So we're agreed."

He nodded. "I'll do anything for you, babe."

"No matter what challenges I set?"

"Challenges?"

"Of course," she answered. "It's a test, remember?"

"I remember. And I'm ready for your challenges — whatever they are."

Now that she'd convinced him, Andi felt shaky inside. She wondered if Sean really understood what she wanted. He probably didn't have any idea of the kind of challenges she'd think up. She wasn't sure herself, but it would be more than sharing chores and making love.

In fact, Andi admitted to herself, she longed for a deep, all-consuming intimacy, a closeness she'd never known before, certainly not with Sean. Now maybe it would be possible for them. With all her heart she hoped so.

At that instant, she knew how passionately she wanted him to pass her test.

While she'd been lost in her hopeful thoughts, Sean had stood up, quickly, before she could stop him. He moved beside her and held out his hand. "Shall we shake on it?"

"Sure." She put her hand in his, and a year of memories grabbed her heart as tightly as his fingers entwined with hers. They weren't the memories of loneliness in foreign cities, but those of homecoming and lovemaking.

As he curved his fingers possessively around hers, Andi was drawn into his smoky gaze. The intensity and longing she saw there caused her heart to flutter wildly. Suddenly he dropped her hand and for an instant they were out of touch. Then he let his fingers brush her cheek. The touch was like a hot flame searing her skin.

"I never stopped wanting you, Andi. Not for one minute. So many nights I've lain awake fantasizing about you, imagining you in my bed—" He moved his hand slowly, letting it drift along her cheek, her chin, to the hollow in her throat. "You're my wife, and I love you," he said softly.

He *would* have to say that word, the very one she'd secretly longed to hear. Even though she knew love was more than a word, just hearing it on his lips comforted her, especially when her pent-up needs had begun to sweep through her, melting away doubts and uncertainty. She'd been so lonely. She'd missed him terribly...

With a soft cry of acquiescence, she stepped into his arms.

He held her closely, cradling her head with his hand. It felt so good to be in his arms. So good that she wondered how she ever could have thought she was over him. She'd lied to herself. Now she knew that whatever their problems, the magic was still there, strong and powerful, an unwavering flame.

Slowly, deliberately, he tilted her head and kissed her. Instinctively, she closed her eyes and let the heat flood through her. It was intense, just as his lips on hers and his tongue invading her mouth, exploring, caressing.

It was all so familiar and at the same time new and different and infinitely more thrilling than she remembered. Deep inside, she felt a melting sensation, smooth and thick as warm honey. That's when she responded.

She slipped her arms around his neck and hungrily pressed her lips to his, mating their tongues.

She moved against him, and Sean felt the outline of her breasts, her pelvis, her thighs. There was an innocent abandon in her motion that nearly caused him to lose control. He could have crushed her in his arms, his need was so great. Instead, he forced himself to move slowly, sliding his hands under her shirt, gliding over the smooth skin.

When he cupped her breasts, her sharp intake of breath fanned the flames of his need. Her nipples were taut and hard against his hands, her breasts smooth as silk. He pushed her back gently against the screen door, and his hand fumbled at the knob. When it opened, they almost fell into the kitchen.

He kicked the door closed behind them and in one motion pulled the big shirt over her head and tossed it on the floor. Then he put his arms around her bottom and lifted her onto the kitchen table.

"Sean, the kitchen . . . in broad daylight—"

"It's either here or on the porch. I'll never make it to the bedroom," he told her as he struggled with her jeans, pulling them down over her knees, a smile curving his lips as he discovered she wore nothing beneath the jeans.

She sat on the edge of the table, wondering how this could happen, *if* it could happen, when he opened her legs gently with his hands and leaned over her. As he pressed against her, Andi wrapped her legs around him. He enclosed her in his arms, his hungry mouth on hers.

With one hand he reached behind her and pushed aside the coffee cup she'd left there. It teetered on the edge of the table before crashing to the floor. His mouth hadn't left hers, and his hands still roamed over her bare thighs.

For Andi, the pleasure of his hands and mouth was indescribable. There was no reality but the throbbing ache inside and the damp heat of her body against him. He lifted her slightly and pressed her back until she was completely stretched out. In one movement he was on the table with her, above her, leaning over and kissing her again. She felt his day's growth of beard rough against her face. Then his fingers found the softness between her legs, the moistness that she knew was there. She heard his sigh of delight at the discovery.

She insinuated her hands between them and felt the hardness of his erection. Fumbling, she unzipped his pants, put her hand inside and freed his manhood, sliding her hand along the hard length of him, caressing with greedy fingers.

Sean gasped with pleasure, and the sound caused her to smile. As they hungrily drank of each other's mouths and fingered those intimate places, the desire became overwhelming.

"I can't wait, Andi," he whispered in a voice husky and rough with passion.

Neither could she.

She lifted her hips and guided him inside. His hardness filled her slowly, fully. It was ecstasy. It was heaven. She opened for him, moving with him, inviting him into her life.

The wooden table creaked beneath them as they moved in unison. His thrusts were as powerful as her heartbeat. Then faster and faster, the friction created between them was hot and electric. It sparked and crackled around them.

She clutched his damp shoulders and felt the muscles strain so tightly she thought they would erupt beneath her fingers. With equal force she felt her breath come in short, ragged bursts as if her heart would explode and her lungs burst. Through the hot blur of her desire, she opened her eyes and saw his face come into focus, her lover, her husband!

Pleasure and desire merged into a crescendo that pushed them to the edge of ecstasy. With dual cries they were rocked by the intensity of climaxes that sent long, shuddering spasms over their bodies in undulating waves of heat.

Sean turned and pulled Andi on top of him. They clung to each other for a long time, muscles quivering, hearts pounding, damp skin pressed against damp skin. Finally their hearts slowed and muscles relaxed.

He turned toward her and realized they were dangerously near the edge of the table. He began to laugh. She joined in the laughter as he sat up, swung his legs off the table and lifted her onto his lap.

"Like old times, eh, babe?"

It was like old times, the two of them, making love in the most unusual places, at any hour of the night and day. "Like old times and more." She laughed again as she slid off his lap until her feet touched the floor. She leaned over, struggling to pull up her jeans. But as she reached for her shirt, he caught her hand.

"You won't be needing that."

She looked at him questioningly.

He jumped from the table and scooped her into his arms. "I suppose there's a bed in this house."

She rested her head against his shoulder and snuggled into the comfort of his body. Her skin tingled everywhere they touched. "Several," she replied.

"Good. Then we have a choice." He strode through the door into the hallway, stopping at the bottom of the stairs. There he kissed her full and thoroughly, and to Andi's disbelief she felt another powerful surge of desire sweep through her.

"Hurry, darling," she murmured. "My room is the closest. At the top of the stairs."

3

ANDI OPENED HER EYES and saw Sean through the curtain of her tangled hair. He had just stepped out of the shower, pulled on a pair of shorts and looped a towel around his neck. He looked damp and delicious.

Squinting, she was able to make out the droplets of water that glistened in his tawny hair and across his tanned, muscular chest. As he dried his hair with one end of the towel, muscles rippled along his shoulders and arms.

Andi sighed, pretty sure he'd guessed that she was awake and decided to strike a provocative pose. It worked, sending tingles from her hairline to her toes and bringing memories of the night before. She sighed again, and this time he heard her.

"Good morning, sleepyhead." He sat beside her on the edge of the bed and leaned forward to kiss her. "I thought I'd let you sleep in." He pushed the tangles of brown hair from her face and let his finger drift along her cheek. She reached for his hand and held on tightly. It felt so damned good to be connected to Sean again.

"You look beautiful this morning," he said.

She smiled. Under his gaze, even this early in the morning, she *felt* beautiful.

"Good enough to eat." He nibbled at her earlobe.

"You look awfully good yourself," she said with the trace of a smile.

He kissed the corner of her mouth, and her smile widened. "Spend the day with me?" he asked.

"That's very enticing." She raised her eyes to meet his, and got caught in their smoky, silvery depths. "But . . ." The heat emanating from his body began to melt her resolve. "I need to get to the store," she managed. "There's a lot to do before we take off for Pawlie's Island tomorrow."

"Tomorrow?"

"Why not?"

"Well, I thought that we—"

She saw where that idea was going. "No, we aren't delaying the marriage test," she said firmly. "The sooner we get to Pawlie's Island the better. Unless you have other plans?" Could he have invented a sudden emergency to postpone the test?

"No plans but you, babe, starting with—breakfast in bed."

She stretched out lazily. "Sorry, I'm not in the mood to cook."

"Maybe I am."

She looked startled. "You?"

"Why not? Okay, the old Sean might've had a problem. But the new guy's ready to take your order."

"Really? Then I'll have—eggs Benedict, French toast, freshly squeezed juice, raspberries and cream—"

"Um, sure. It may take a little time, but—" He headed for the door, determined.

She laughed. "Coffee and toast will be fine," she called to his retreating back.

"Not for the wife of Sean Fleming," came the reply.

She snuggled into her pillows and hugged herself with satisfaction. It had been wonderful going to bed with Sean, loving him, waking up in his arms. She let her mind dwell on the night before. He still owned the title of world's most passionate lover. But there was so much more. Sean was generous and giving, romantic and inventive, and their lovemaking was totally satisfying. If only the rest of their lives could be as good as their sex lives.

This was what they did best. But they couldn't seem to build a lasting foundation on that extraordinary passion. Maybe the marriage test, as ridiculous as it seemed, would be the turning point. Sean had some relationship problems, no doubt about it. But then she wasn't Miss Perfect. The test could be the answer.

She decided to get serious and come up with a *real* marriage test. She rummaged in the drawer of the bedside table, found a yellow pad and pen and began to scribble her ideas. The sound of crashing pots from below barely interrupted her concentration. She was on a roll, buoyed by Sean's cheerful shouts that all was well.

She was still jotting down her ideas when he appeared at the door with a tray and a pleased smirk.

"Voilà, mam'selle. Here ees your breakfast," he announced in an atrocious French accent. He moved to the side of the bed and whipped back the napkin that covered the tray. "Not just coffee and toast, but coffee, toast—and cereal!" He deposited the tray on her lap. "All natural and healthy and . . . room temperature. I forgot and made the toast a little early," he confessed.

She bit off a corner. "I happen to love cold toast, darling. Besides, it's the thought that counts." She glanced at the cereal, soggy and swimming in too much milk. Avoiding it, she took another bite of toast.

He waited patiently for her reaction, and she rewarded him with a buttery kiss. His lips lingered on hers. "We could skip breakfast, go back to bed . . ."

The tray swayed dangerously. Andi steadied the dishes—and her husband. "I have to get to the store, remember? You can come with me," she offered.

"Oh, thanks," he said. "Just the way I was hoping to spend the morning. At the store. About as interesting as—" He picked up her list from the bedside table. "Reading a grocery list. Except..." He paused and looked it over. "This isn't about groceries."

"Nope. It's our marriage test."

"You can't be serious, babe. You've written the damned thing down?"

"You bet I have. I've never been more serious in my life. Unless we have it in black and white, we can't be sure of the outcome."

He settled on the bed. "Is this like the Olympics? Do I get rated from one to ten?"

She snuggled beside him. At the moment, it was all still a game, but the time would come—in the next few days—when they would enter into the test seriously. "I hadn't thought of a rating system, but it's not a bad idea." At his offended look, she assured him, "I'm just joking, Sean. The list is a guide to the areas we need to concentrate on—"

"God, you make this sound so damned clinical, Andi. We're talking about us, me and you. Our marriage. Our love." He put away the pad. "How can you measure love?"

"I can think of a hundred ways," she said slowly. "Kindness and thoughtfulness and caring and—but the list is a little more specific and, well, behavior oriented. Sometimes actions *do* speak louder than words."

She ignored Sean's groan and went on. "I've thought of three major areas that should be a test for any marriage. I'm sure they'd be on everyone's list."

"If everyone made a list," he said. "Which, I might remind you, no one does." Grudgingly he picked up the pad again. "Number one, food. Under that, let's see, we have planning, shopping, preparation. Haven't I already passed the preparation part?"

Andi tried not to make a face. "The idea is consistency, Sean. Anyone can pull off a . . . meal—" she glanced at the soggy cereal and tried not to stumble on the word "—but we're talking about the long haul. I don't intend to do all the cooking," she added.

"'Course not," he agreed. "That wouldn't be fair at all. This is the nineties, and men and women share. Even the cooking."

"Especially the cooking," she added with a nudge.

"Yes, especially." He went back to the list. "Topic number two, cleaning and repairs. Now that sounds more like a guy thing. The repairs part. Do I get a hammer and saw, or how about a tool belt?"

"I don't know about the belt, but I'm sure there are tools at the cottage. We'll have plenty to do."

"I can't wait," he muttered. "Now let's get to number three, rhythm of marriage." He frowned and threw her a sideways look. "I don't imagine this rhythm has anything to do with making love?"

She shook her head. "Not exactly the way you mean it, but all relationships have to do with love, don't they? By rhythm I mean how we operate during the day when we're not doing chores, how we spend our leisure time. Do we share hobbies and interests? Is it possible for us just to *be* together, all day, every day, with no outside diversions?"

"Andi, of course—"

"It may sound obvious, even silly to you, but it's important to have this time alone to figure out what we have and what we want—from each other."

His voice was soft and silky. "I know what I want. I want you."

"Sean, I have the same feelings, and you know it. But I'm not talking about sex. I want a marriage, a real one. This is a test for me, too. After two weeks on Pawlie's Island, we'll both have a better understanding of who we are and where we're going."

"And where are you going, Andi?" He put his hand on her shoulder, letting it linger there a moment before tracing a lazy path down her arm. Andi knew she could get caught up in his seductive mood, and if that could happen here it could happen on the island. It was time to get down to business.

"I'm going to the store, Sean," she said firmly as she scooted to the edge of the bed. "Why don't you join Pam and me for lunch?"

That sounded pretty uninteresting to Sean, who immediately said, "Sounds fascinating." Then he added with a boyish grin, "Want me to shop for the groceries and prepare the meal?" Too late. Andi had already disappeared into the bathroom.

Sean checked his watch and realized his network's newscast was coming up. He grabbed the television remote control and clicked it on. Nothing happened. He hit the button again, cursed to himself, then got up and flicked the switch on the set. A blank screen looked back at him.

"Hey, what's the matter with the TV?" he called out. "I wanted to catch the news." Twelve hours without news was a lifetime to Sean.

She stuck her head out the bathroom door. "It's broken, and I haven't had time to get it repaired." Then she grinned and added, "Now's a good time to start getting used to being newless. There's no television on Pawlie's Island."

"Doesn't bother me one bit, babe," he lied. "All my time will be devoted to you." As soon as he heard the shower running, he added, "And finding a way around this damned marriage test."

ANDI UNLOCKED THE STORE and stood for a moment in the dim light. She had to admit it, Kent Unlimited was a homey place. She was going to miss it. The store was open from ten in the morning until eight at night, six days a week. Her father had spent much of his time in the store. It was his avocation as well as his vocation. It was his happiness, next to his wife and children—maybe even before them. His father started it as a small shop for sportsmen, selling fishing and hunting supplies, more than sixty-five years before, and he took over with enthusiasm. There'd never been the slightest doubt that Kent Unlimited would remain in the family and grow.

Andi and Pam had worked there on weekends and during summer vacations. It was expected. They never had much choice, but as far as Andi was concerned, it was time for the family business to be handed over—at a good price—to another family. Pam might not agree in theory, but in reality, as a wife and expectant mother, she had very little choice.

Ten minutes to go before the doors opened, and the store was pleasantly quiet without the customers browsing among the summer sale items or hovering around the colorful T-shirt counter. Andi moved along the aisles of half-price skis and parkas to the new displays of woven hammocks and summer picnic baskets, feeling a momentary pang of nostalgia. A lot of years had gone into making Kent Unlimited the area's most successful outfitter.

Before she had a chance to get teary, Andi called out, "Pam, I'm here."

There was an answering call from the rear of the store. "We're in the office. Come and join us."

"Who's we?" Andi asked, heading toward the office.

Pam stepped through the door, and a stocky, dark haired man appeared beside her. "It's me," he announced. "Just thought I'd drop in and see how you're doing."

"Mike!" Andi held out her arms in welcome. "I can't believe it. What brings you up here?"

He enveloped her in a bear hug. "I was just sailing by..."

At her quizzical look, he explained. "I've been vacationing on my boat and decided to spend a little time exploring a seaside town." He laughed. "And I just happened to choose Clarion. Actually, it was an excuse to pursue you."

"Pursue?"

He laughed. "I'm still trying to get you to come to work for me. His dark eyes glittered mischievously. "Did you forget?"

"No, of course not."

"Maybe when your husband came back, you got sidetracked."

Pam suddenly seemed to come alive. "It's ten o'clock. Time to open up." She disappeared quickly, leaving Andi staring after her with a frown.

Mike stepped into the office and Andi followed, still wondering at Pam's sudden disappearance.

The office had remained unchanged over the years except for the accumulation of more stuff. That's what their father had called it, affectionately. There were boxes of old tin containers from the thirties, the store's first catalogs, rough mock-ups of the original T-shirt design—all the memorabilia from decades of success. After his death, neither Andi nor Pam had the heart to throw anything away, so they'd just crowded another desk into the room between the file cabinets, balanced the telephone and fax machine on top and managed to keep going.

Seated at one of the desks, Mike picked up a screwdriver and began to take apart the answering machine.

"What are you doing?" Andi asked.

He looked up with a smile. "Playing handyman. Pam said this wasn't working, so I volunteered to fix it." He opened the machine, quickly examined the wiring, made an adjustment and put it together. The whole operation took about forty seconds. Then he looked at her, raised an eyebrow and asked, "So how's it going with Sean?"

She was still ogling his rapid repair. "Did you fix it?"

He plugged the machine in and pressed a button. "You've reached Kent Unlimited. The store is now closed. Please leave a message and we'll return your call during the next working day." He waited, hit another button and listened as the recording repeated. "It seems okay, but we'll have to have someone call in to make sure." Then he smiled at Andi. "Now, about Sean."

She laughed. "You're amazing. As for Sean, he's fine."

"And you?"

"I'm fine, too," she replied. "Sean wants us to get back together, and I want the same thing." She sat at her desk. "That's why I can't give you an answer right now about the job, Mike. I want to work for TSS, but I have to give my marriage a second chance."

Mike leaned back at the other desk and nodded thoughtfully. "I wouldn't expect anything less of you,

Andi. However, I think you'll have a tremendous future with us, and I'm willing to wait, at least a while longer." He paused dramatically. "And from what I've heard about the freewheeling Sean Fleming, he'll never pass that marriage test. From foreign correspondent to Mr. Housewife? It doesn't compute."

Andi's eyes widened in disbelief, and for a moment she was speechless. Finally, the words came out in a sputtering rush. "She told you? Pam actually told you about the marriage test? I can't believe she'd do that!" Her anger swelled. What was Pam thinking of to talk to Mike about *her* marriage?

Mike leaned toward her. "Hey, don't be upset. She wasn't gossiping. I asked how you were, she mentioned Sean, and it just went from there." He reached for her arm. "I'm a friend, Andi. You know you can trust me."

"Of course I can, and I realize this isn't your fault, but—" She pulled away. "Well, dammit, Pam talks too much. God knows who she'll tell next. My friends, *her* friends, some customer walking into the store. I'm going to put a stop to this right now."

Andi whirled and strode out of the office into the store. Pam was at the cash register, chatting with a customer as she bagged his purchase of Hug-a-Moose T-shirts for his entire family. Andi resisted the urge to blast her sister in front of the customer and bided her time among the rows of running shoes and hiking boots, seething. Pam glanced at her as if she knew what was coming.

SEAN WOKE SUDDENLY to the phone ringing. Damn, he'd agreed to meet Andi for lunch. He glanced at the clock—ten past one. He rolled over and picked up the insistent phone.

"Hi, babe. Sorry I overslept—"

"You don't have to apologize to me, darling. Just don't call me babe."

He sat up with a grin. "Reena, how did you know I was here?"

"A mother knows these things, son." Her voice floated over the wires like warm cream. "I called your office in New York, and they told me you'd headed to Maine. So tell me. How is Andrea?"

He heard the warmth in his mother's voice fade when she mentioned her daughter-in-law, but he ignored the tone. "She's great. We had a very—satisfying reunion."

"Well. Yes." He could picture her squirming about that. "Then Andrea has gotten over this foolish separation business?"

"Looks like it."

"Thank heavens she's come around. I can't imagine what got into her when she simply abandoned you in Europe. In my time, things were certainly different. I remember following your father from post to post, from—"

Sean held the phone away from his ear while she rattled on. He'd heard the story more times than he cared to remember, a recounting of the years Reena Scott Fleming spent moving with her husband to different Army posts across the United States and in Europe. As she told the story, it had been a wonderful and rewarding life. He suspected a touch of the martyr in all that noise about the duty of following her husband. As he grew older, he began to wonder if the patina of wifely devotion didn't actually hide resentment on the part of his mother for never having had a life of her own.

Even as he listened to her now, at arm's length, he could detect a slight whine that he recognized as dissatisfaction tinged with regret. Five years after her husband's death, Reena was resettled in her home town of Albany, New York, but there was still something unfinished about her, as if she really wasn't sure what to do with the rest of her life, having spent so much of it as another person's appendage.

When she took a breath, Sean jumped into the conversation. "I understand your feelings, Mom. Married couples should be together, and I have great hopes that will be the case with us. I expect Andi will be coming to London with me."

He heard her audible sigh of relief.

"But first, we're going to have a second honeymoon—on a coastal island that belongs to their family." He chuckled. "She's devised some kind of test for me—"

"You can't mean it!" Reena's voice rose half an octave. "What kind of test?"

"Calm down, Mom. It's no big deal. She has an idea I need to prove to her that I can be a good husband."

"I don't like the sound of that. Don't like it at all. It's not a woman's place to demand proof of such things," she commented censoriously.

Sean placated her quickly. "It's no big deal. We're just going to experiment doing things a little differently. It's a new-style marriage."

Reena interrupted. "What's the matter with the old style?"

"Absolutely nothing, Reena." God, why had he ever mentioned the marriage test? He knew why. Because, being Reena, she'd find out about it one way or another. "Listen, Mom, everything's going to work out fine. Andi and I will be together in London, I guarantee."

"All I want is for you to be happy, son. After all, you're my only child—"

Sean grimaced. As if he hadn't heard that all his life. "But I love you enough for twenty kids," he said, repeating the line he'd invented in childhood, the one that melted his mother's heart. As usual, it worked.

"I know you do, darling. Now don't forget to keep in touch."

"I will." He glanced at the clock again. "Have to go now. I'm meeting Andi at the store."

"Give her my love," Reena said, "and tell her that test is ridiculous."

"Don't worry about the test. I'll pass it with flying colors. Remember, I always land on my feet."

Sean left the house with a feeling of optimism, walking the few short blocks to the heart of Clarion almost jauntily. What he'd told Reena was true—the test would be a snap.

Kent Unlimited stood proudly between a pharmacy and a jewelers. Tradition was reflected in the neat gold lettering on the door—Kent Unlimited, Established 1930 by Thomas Kent. Andi's grandfather, he recalled. The family's roots went deep in Clarion. He pushed open the door, stepped inside and came face-to-face with a row of Hug-a-Moose sweatshirts. He smiled in remembrance of his first meeting with Andi.

The hotel bar in Saint Moritz. Andi had been wearing a bright yellow sweatshirt with a red Hug-a-Moose logo. First the shirt caught his attention—and then the woman. They'd laughed about it later, that meeting of eyes across a crowded room that had begun with a company logo.

The woman behind the cash register was a short, brown-eyed blonde, very pregnant and easily identified. "Hello, Pam," he said in a friendly if not brotherly voice. He held that tone back, just as he did an urge to give his sister-in-law a hug. With any encouragement, he would have grabbed her affectionately, but he could read women, and clearly, this one wouldn't be thrilled by the gesture. So he held out his hand. "I'm Sean."

She smiled. If you could call the expression a smile. "I recognize you," she said. "From TV. Andi told me you'd be coming by for lunch. But you're late so I went ahead and ordered sandwiches. You're welcome to join us."

"Yeah, thanks. Sorry about being late but I overslept." He decided to give it one more try. "By the way, congratulations on the baby."

She nodded, a little more friendly, he thought as he pressed on. "I bet you're both very pleased, you and—" Sean's mind went blank. What was her husband's name? Keith? No, that wasn't it. Karl? Kit? "You and your husband," he finished lamely.

Pam gave him another smile, chillier this time. "It's Kevin, and I'll tell my sister you're here." She disappeared toward the back of the store.

Damn, Sean thought. Messed up that one. He'd have to come up with a way to get on her good side. Maybe a fabulous gift for the baby—something very expensive.

While he waited for Andi, he checked out the shop, noticed a section of men's sport clothes and rifled through a stack of plaid shirts. Andi slipped up behind him and slid her arms around his waist. "You're late."

"So I've heard," he said. "I overslept. And then Reena called."

"So she found you. I can imagine how that conversation went."

"And you'd be right. But by the time we hung up, she seemed pleased that you and I were working things out. We *are* working things out, aren't we?" He turned and took her in his arms, dropping a kiss on her hair.

"Definitely. Unless you've changed your mind." She looked up at him. "Why're you asking?"

"Your sister."

"Uh-oh. What's she done now?"

"Nothing all that bad. She just greeted me as if I carried bubonic plague."

"Don't take it personally. She's not angry at you. We had a fight. Well, more like a small argument." She decided not to tell him the reason for their disagreement. "It's no problem. Pam's a little uptight these days with the baby coming, my leaving, selling the store...all that." Andi stood on her tiptoes and kissed him. "You understand, don't you?"

"One more kiss, and I will."

It didn't take long for her to agree to that.

His kiss was very thorough and made Andi wish she could change the day's agenda. She'd promised Pam she'd stay at the shop until at least six o'clock. Now she wanted nothing more than to spend the day in bed with her husband.

When the kiss ended, she was secretly pleased to see that Sean's breathing was as ragged as hers. And it turned out that his thoughts were also the same. "Let's skip lunch and go back to bed," he whispered.

It was tempting, but today Pam came first. "I promised Pam. She needs me, Sean." She ran her fingers lightly across his lips. "Be sweet to her, please."

"I'm always sweet, babe." He bent and nuzzled her neck. "And romantic. The sweatshirts on the rack reminded me of Saint Moritz. You were wearing that bright yellow Hug-a-Moose—"

"And you were knee-deep in Euro-ski bunnies."

"But looking at you."

"At my shirt," she corrected.

"You told me you'd designed it for your dad's store, and I thought, 'Now there's a woman with a great sense of humor.'"

"Sometimes," she teased.

"We're going to recapture all the laughter, I guarantee." His lips drifted along her cheek toward her mouth.

She was so into his attentions and her responses to them that she didn't hear Michael come into the store.

"Oh, sorry. I didn't mean to interrupt."

She jumped at the sound of his voice.

He was holding the answering machine and looking embarrassed. Or at least feigning the look. "I thought it was time to try out the machine."

Andi took a step back. Dammit. Pam sent him in, she was sure of that. Or was she being paranoid?

"Oh, Mike. This—this is my husband, Sean Fleming," she babbled.

She looked from one to the other, only to find that they were sizing each other up, like boxers in the ring. Good Lord, what was this? She'd had enough emotional turmoil in the past few hours, and she certainly didn't want a scene in the store.

"Sean," she said quickly, "meet Michael Rossi from TSS. I told you about him."

Right. But she evidently hadn't told him enough. Sean was seeing something else in Mike, a rival. Looking at them, she saw a study in opposites. Sean was tawny and golden, slim and tall. Mike, with his dark hair and eyes, was shorter in stature but had a more muscular build. And each of them possessed a massive ego and an overabundance of self-confidence. She could almost feel the testosterone level rising.

Then Sean set things right, as only he could, with one of his TV interview smiles and the friendly extension of his hand. "Nice to meet you, Rossi," he said as Andi breathed a long sigh of relief. "I hear you've offered my wife a job."

Mike's smile was equally wide—and insincere. "A fantastic job for a fantastic woman." He clasped Sean's hand. Sean winced almost imperceptibly at the pressure but kept the smile in place.

"I don't know about the job, but you're right about the woman. Mike, is it?"

"Yes, *Sean*," Mike said, very satisfied with himself.

"Great offer, Mike." Sean put his arm possessively around Andi and pulled her close. "Too bad she won't be able to accept it, but—"

Mike's eyebrows rose ever so slightly. "Oh, I didn't think she'd come to a decision—"

"Just a minute!" Andi inserted. "*She* is here. Please don't talk about me as if I was in another room. As far as *my* decision, there hasn't been one." She looked at Sean. "None."

He didn't react at all to that remark. Instead, he kissed her cheek and murmured, "But I'm very optimistic." Shifting his gaze to Mike, his eyes challenged. "You may not know this, but Andi and I are going on a second honeymoon to Pawlie's Island."

Andi groaned inwardly and prayed Mike wouldn't announce that he knew about the test. He didn't.

"Pawlie's Island is beautiful in the summer," Mike commented casually.

"You've been there?" There was a touch of jealousy in Sean's voice, and Andi felt him tense.

"Sure." Mike paused long enough for that to sink in before adding, "At least, I've been close. I'm a sailor, and I've seen the island from my boat. I'd like to explore it sometime. Looks interesting. A little primitive," he added, and Andi couldn't help but wonder if that had been done on purpose, to irritate Sean who was clearly not the primitive type.

"Mike just fixed the answering machine for us," she said, deliberately changing the topic. "Why don't I go next door and call over here—see if it's working?"

"No, I'll go," Mike offered.

"It's okay, Rossi," Sean said easily. "You and Andi work out the phone problem. I'm going to the office to have a sandwich and get to know my sister-in-law."

Sean walked toward the back. He didn't like the idea of leaving them alone, but Andi was getting uptight. Probably unhappy with his possessive act. It *had* been a bit macho, he admitted to himself, a sort of Me-Tarzan-You-Jane thing. But, dammit, he wasn't about to be charming while Rossi showed off his repair skills and boasted about his sailing. He'd charm Pam instead.

He paused at the office door. "I heard there were sandwiches back here."

"Lobster salad. And iced tea." Pam pushed the box of sandwiches toward him.

Sean sat down, unwrapped one and took a big bite. "This is great. Fresh lobster?"

"Sure," she said curtly.

"Will we be able to get lobster on the island?"

"If you ask the fishermen to drop some off. There are lots of traps out there."

"Great," he said, adding quickly, "I'm looking forward to the next two weeks."

"Mmm." It was just a noise, not even an acknowledging one, he thought. Idle conversation was getting him nowhere so he opted for another tack, leaning forward, meeting her brown eyes directly. His voice was low and sincere. "I know this isn't easy on you, my appearing out of nowhere and spiriting Andi away, just when the baby's due and the store's going up for sale."

"About the store," she said, "that's still up in the air. Very much so," she added almost defiantly.

Sean nodded. "I can understand that it's a hard decision." For an instant he thought he saw a tear glimmer in her eye, and he felt suddenly sorry for her. "Pam, I can see what you're going through, and I want you to know that I'd like us to be friends. You have enough worries, and I don't want you to be concerned about your sister. You love her very much, but so do I. I'll take care of her."

"But will you make her happy?"

He was surprised by the directness of the question. "I'm damn well going to try. These two weeks are a kind of—well, a test for us, and I have great hopes."

Pam seemed to drop her defenses. "Well, maybe things will work out for the best."

"No maybes about it," he said. "This second honeymoon is going to be all we've hoped for—and more."

The phone rang just then, but when Pam reached for it, he cautioned, "They're testing the answering machine that Mr. Fixit worked on, so don't answer."

"Mr. Fixit," she repeated, offering her first real smile. "You're jealous! Well, there's no reason. Andi isn't interested in Mike *that* way, believe me."

"Good," Sean said, "because I'm the only man in her life for now—and in the future."

SEAN DRAGGED a crate of wine from the car and lugged it into the house, adding it to the other supplies he'd bought for their sojourn on Pawlie's Island. He'd hung around Kent Unlimited until Mike took off, deciding he wasn't going to let the guy have the last word with Andi, and then he'd driven to Bangor to shop. Which was fine with Andi. In fact, she'd been pleased when he volunteered to handle one of the items on her crazy list and take charge of all the food for their two-week stay. Even Pam seemed impressed, but that didn't surprise Sean. She was definitely softening toward him.

He felt pretty damned good about himself, too.

He slipped a bottle of champagne into the fridge alongside the two steamed lobsters he'd picked up on the way home. He had it all planned. Their last night in Clarion was going to be the best ever.

He took the steps to the second floor two at a time, whistling happily, wheeled into the bedroom and stopped. The TV screen stared blankly at him. "Damn," he said aloud, remembering the busted set. "What I need now is Mr. Fixit." The answering machine had worked perfectly, and Rossi had puffed up like a rooster at his success. In Sean's opinion, Andi and Pam had overdone their thanks. But he could use the guy now; no doubt about that.

He flicked the remote control, hoping for a miracle. Nothing. He checked the plug. He thumped the back of the set with the palm of his hand. That about exhausted his fix-it abilities. But not quite. There was one foolproof way to get the TV repaired.

The phone book was on the desk. He thumbed through quickly to the television section. Then he picked up the phone and punched in the numbers.

"Hi, I have an emergency. I'll pay double time if you can get a repairman here in the next half hour to fix my TV."

4

SEAN HAD IT ALL DOWN. This TV repair stuff was a cinch, especially with good instructions. Confidently, he repeated the ones he'd been given to finish the job.

"Replace the back of the set and tighten the mounting screws with a Phillips head screwdriver." He'd known what that was, of course, but he didn't carry one around and had no idea where to look in the house.

The television repairman, overwhelmed with the amount of money Sean was willing to pay for a simple circuit repair, had gladly left a screwdriver behind for him. Hardly a gift, Sean had thought as he'd looked at the bill and written out the huge check.

Now, standing jauntily behind the set, the screwdriver held loosely in his hand, he went through the rest of his drill.

"Reconnect the antenna wires." That part wasn't hard. He'd played around with camera hookups and VCRs for years, but the actual repairing of equipment was beyond his skills. That had been left to the experts. Now it was left to him to put on the finishing touches just as Andi got home.

He checked his watch. Almost six. She should be walking through the door any minute. He adjusted the table lamp to illuminate his working area and crouched on the floor. As if on cue, the front door opened.

"Sean! I'm home—finally," she called out.

"Up here, babe. I'm almost finished."

When he heard her footsteps on the stairs, he connected the wires and moved on to the final step. "Reattach the cable."

The timing was perfect. Andi opened the door and stopped in her tracks, stunned. He had to force himself to keep from breaking up, her puzzlement was so obvious.

"What in the world—"

He waited a beat before answering. "Keep your fingers crossed, babe. I think I'll have this under control in a minute." He went to work with his screwdriver. Out of the corner of his eye, he could see Andi's look of amazement.

She sank down on the bed, watching. "Where did you find a screwdriver? I wouldn't have known where to look for Dad's tools."

"There was a toolbox in my rental car." That was probably true, Sean thought, a little pang of conscience preventing him from saying he actually *found* the screwdriver there. He got to his feet with exaggerated casualness. "Grab the remote, babe. Let's see if this thing works."

Andi hit the power button. Images of the local news team filled the screen, and the audio followed immediately. She signaled her delight. "Darling, this is wonderful! I had no idea—"

"Didn't you?" he asked innocently. "Can't imagine why not. I've been around high tech equipment for years, Andi. A guy picks up things." He tried to keep his smile modest as he sat beside her on the bed. "And this is a freebie, babe, not even part of the test. I just wanted to show you that I may be a newsman, but I have a few things in common with Rossi, your Mr. Fixit." He had some trouble keeping the hostility out of his voice. "I'm just as handy to have around."

She cupped his face in her hands. "There's no one else I want to have around—ever."

Her lips were warm and sweet on his, causing Sean to instantly forget about Mr. Fixit or anyone else but Andi. He tasted her with his tongue, exploring the softness of her mouth. He felt her melt against him, and his blood began to pound slowly, powerfully, filling him with longing. He lay back and pulled Andi on top of him. "Do I get a reward for being such a good boy?"

"Sure. And if you'll just give me a little time, I'll try to think what that could be," she added in a teasing voice, planting another kiss on his lips. "I have an idea," she whispered. "How about if I take you out to dinner?"

He stayed steady enough to answer. "You'll have to think of something else, babe. I've taken care of the dinner thing. It's in the fridge. Lobster and champagne—"

She planted a series of kisses along his cheek and chin. "You do think of everything, don't you?"

"If it pleases you, I'm for it. All I want to do is make you happy, babe." He tightened his arms around her, pressing her warmth against his burgeoning arousal. She squirmed delightfully, which sent another tremor of desire stabbing through him.

It also triggered a fabulous memory. He filled his hands with her hair and whispered against her ear, "Remember that afternoon in Málaga when it was so hot—"

"And the hotel had no air-conditioning—" She joined in the memory game while still responding to the here-and-now of his warm breath against her cheek. "The sun was a huge red ball in the sky. We closed the blinds to keep it out."

"And ordered two bottles of icy cold champagne from room service," he continued.

"Then undressed and poured all that bubbly over each other to cool off." Andi giggled at the memory. "And then we—" She paused to kiss him again, running her tongue around his lips and then dipping inside his mouth.

Sean's voice was a murmur of sensuality. "What did we do next?" he asked.

"You remember," she said. "We did something delicious . . ."

"Oh, yeah. We licked the champagne off each other."

"Before we . . ." With a low whimper of anticipation, Andi reached for the zipper of Sean's trousers. The hot passion of memory merged with the heated flow of her present need. They'd been apart so long, and she realized only now how starved she'd been for his love—and his lovemaking.

"Before we what, Andi?"

She answered with her body, responding to him, opening, softening. She was dazed and light-headed, captured by his touch, his scent, his taste. Everything inside her seemed to melt, just as it had that day beneath the blazing Spanish sun.

His hand pulled at the buttons of her blouse, and his mouth greedily sought hers. As they struggled from their clothes, she managed one more muffled sentence.

"Turn off the TV, Sean. Tonight we'll make our own news."

SEAN WAS FIRST out of the little skiff when Ed Ennis tied up at the wharf on Pawlie's Island. He'd thoroughly enjoyed crossing the channel in the small boat with Andi beside him, laughing, the wind in her hair. He hadn't even minded the less than hospitable presence of the skipper.

How long had it been since he'd taken a ride in a small boat on a windy day? Once, as a young reporter, he'd crowded into a boat about this size filled with freedom fighters; another time, he'd floated alone, hidden in the bottom of such a boat to escape enemy bullets. But he couldn't remember a peaceful boating experience.

This one had been exhilarating.

"Toss me up those duffel bags," he called to Andi. "Then Ed and I can unload the supplies."

He stacked the canvas bags filled with their clothes and bedding on the dock and gave Andi a hand out of the skiff.

"Isn't this fantastic?" she exclaimed. "I'd forgotten how much I love the island."

Sean took a quick look around. A rocky beach crept out into the wave-tossed bay. Pine trees clung to the jagged shoreline and seemed to cover the rest of the island, which looked wild and deserted. It wasn't his fantasy island of sugar-white sands and beach cabanas. But in a way it was interesting. Primitive didn't have to be all bad. Luxury could wait. Hell, it would have to. The test was about to begin.

Andi was still waxing rhapsodic about the island. "The eastern side of Pawlie's is much wilder," she said, "with high, rocky cliffs. But you'll see. We'll have a chance to explore it all, and you're going to love it."

The wind whipped her shiny brown hair around her head and pinkened her cheeks. Sean couldn't resist. He took her in his arms and kissed her. She clung to him, laughing, until Ed's nasal twang interrupted.

"If you lovebirds will excuse me, I got lobster traps to check before dark, and I need some help, young feller, with these boxes of yours. What you got in them? Gold bullion?"

"Not quite," Sean said with a laugh, thinking that what *was* in the boxes was almost as expensive. He kept the contents to himself as he took the first crate Ed lifted and handed to him easily.

Mocking the sailor's style, he reached out, grabbed the box—and almost fell on his face. The lobsterman was short and wiry but obviously as strong as a bull. Sean grimaced, set his legs and with a struggle managed not to drop the damned thing.

He'd packed the boxes, but Ed had loaded them on the boat, and as far as Sean was concerned, once the stuff was on the deck, the rest was up to Ed. Who had other plans.

"Gotta go now," he declared.

"But what about—" Sean began.

"Don't worry, darling," Andi advised. "There's a wheelbarrow in the toolshed."

Sean heaved a sigh of relief as Ed settled his brimmed cap low on his forehead. "Then I'll be off. Time is money," he added, fixing his steely blue eyes purposefully on Sean.

Taking the hint, Sean reached into his pocket and handed over a couple of bills, which Ed took with a nod of thanks.

"You'll be dropping off some lobsters for us, right?" Sean asked. When he didn't get an immediate response, he added, "Remember, Pam mentioned that when you unloaded the traps—"

"Mebbe I will . . ." Ed got into the skiff, and squinting into the sun, untied the hawser. "And mebbe I won't." He pushed off. "It all depends." The little boat began its putt-putt across the bay, and Ed turned toward the open water, obviously without another thought.

Sean looked at Andi, who shrugged. "That's Ed for you. But I have a feeling he'll drop the lobster off. He likes to live up to his contrary image."

"Well, I'm just as glad he's taken his contrary image and departed the scene. Because," he said, "now we're . . . alone at last!" He laughed and gave her a big hug. "Come on, babe, and show me our love nest."

"HERE IT IS," Andi said, proudly dropping her knapsack at the bottom of the steps. "Our family cottage." She shot Sean a curious look and reacted to his expression with an explanation. "I told you it was a little primitive."

"It's charming," he answered honestly. "Like something out of the Black Forest."

While she tried to figure out whether that was a plus or a negative, she watched him take everything in.

The log cabin was at the edge of a clearing, tucked in among towering pines. Their scent was sharp and sweet on the morning air. She thought it was a wonderful sight, with the sun making darting patterns of light and shade across the peaked roof. She wasn't sure what Sean thought.

They climbed the steps to the wide planked porch, and Andi pushed open the door with a grin. "No locks needed on our island."

Sean followed her inside, and she could feel his eyes taking in the scene as they adjusted from sunlight to shadow. She walked to the huge stone fireplace, which dominated one end of the room, and stood beside one of the mismatched sofas.

She looked at him.

"It's...homey," he said, and she tried not to laugh. It wouldn't do to be amused at what was clearly his cynicism.

"There's just this one big room downstairs," she explained as she opened the windows and pushed back the shutters to let in the sun. "Except for a little kitchen and storage area."

"Bedroom?" he asked.

"Three of them. Upstairs," she added.

"One's enough," he said, but she'd moved on, pausing at the kitchen door. "I did tell you no electricity, didn't I?"

"You said no TV but didn't mention electricity. There's not even a generator?"

"Nope. And we have to draw water from the well and heat it over the fire." She let that sink in and, noting his somber expression, added, "But there is a shortwave radio somewhere. In the closet, I think." Then, putting her hands on her hips, she surveyed the room with pleasure. "So, what do you think?"

"I'm a field reporter, babe. I'm used to roughing it." Then he looked around and noticed the spiderwebs, the smell of mildew, the dust motes floating in the air.

"Looks like we need to clean up a little," she said.

"Looks like it," he agreed as he wrote his initials, entwined with hers, in the dust on the long wood table.

"As soon as we wheel the stuff up from the dock, we'll get to work. There are a lot of cleaning supplies here. I'm sort of looking forward to seeing you sporting a broom and mop. I think I'll dig out the camera and take a picture of that."

If she thought that would put him off, she was wrong. He quickly got into the spirit, flexing his arm. "I'm ready and willing, babe." He took her in his arms. "You might think I'm a softy, but you'll find out differently when we get down to the hard work. I haven't forgotten our deal, Andi."

She hugged him hard. "Neither have I. And we're off to a good start."

Sean threw back his head and laughed. "Ten minutes on the island and no arguments yet." He whirled her around and deposited her at the door. "Let's start at the beginning. Point me in the direction of the wheelbarrow, and I'll bring up our supplies."

"I'll help," she told him. "After all, this is a joint effort. There's no job that's strictly male or female. You'll find that out when we start cleaning."

He followed her down the steps. "Do I get graded for each task, or will it be cumulative?" he teased.

"Both," she called over her shoulder.

Catching up with her, he asked, "And how about my remuneration?"

"That depends."

He stopped short and grabbed her hand. "Wait a minute. I'll work hard, but you've gotta dangle some sort of carrot in front of me."

"I'll think about that," she decided, moving on.

The shed was behind the house at the end of the path. She pulled open the door and waited for the expected rustling noises. They came immediately as unknown critters reacted to the intrusion and scurried away. She looked at Sean, who made a face but didn't comment.

Andi pointed in the direction of the wheelbarrow, buried beneath a stack of lumber. "First things first."

"What about that carrot?"

"At the end of the workday."

He dumped out the planks and pulled the wheelbarrow free. "No rewards as we go along?"

"Work first, and then play. We won't have the sunlight forever."

He let out an exaggerated sigh. "Has anyone ever told you that you're far too organized?"

"Constantly."

"And much too sensible?"

"Of course. Isn't that one of the reasons you love me?"

"It must be one. I just didn't know it until now," he answered.

A FAMILY OF FIELD MICE had made themselves at home in one of the overstuffed chairs, and a canopy of spiderwebs covered the ceiling corners. But after a few hours, Andi and Sean had made headway against the months of neglect.

They'd worked side by side, he with broom and mop, she with dust cloths and damp sponges. They'd stopped once for ham and cheese sandwiches and beer that Sean had brought in an ice-filled cooler. She was thankful for the ice and sorry that by nightfall it would be gone, but that was one of the challenges of island life, making the best of what was there. Andi's family had always used the cabin as a getaway to a life that was simple, uncomplicated and basic. But because their sojourns had been more frequent, clean-up time had been swift, and all four family members had pitched in.

It took Andi and Sean a little longer, but soon the kitchen sink was scrubbed and scoured, the floors mopped, and it was time to put out fresh towels and make up the bed in the largest bedroom.

But it wasn't time to get in it, Andi had to remind Sean.

"Just for an hour or two? Or even a few minutes," he suggested, nuzzling her neck below the scarf she'd tied around her head.

"As long as there's daylight we need to take advantage..."

"I'm taking advantage," he said as he turned her just enough to plant a kiss on the corner of her mouth.

She kissed him back quickly. "I'll pick the wildflowers for the table tonight," she said, "and I promise a wonderfully romantic evening, dinner by candlelight..."

Sean wiped the perspiration from his forehead, leaving a dark smudge of dirt. "As soon as the sun goes down, we'll be doing *everything* by candlelight," he quipped. "By the way, how do we cook around here?"

"Didn't you see the wood-burning stove in the kitchen?"

He had, but had tried to ignore it.

"Or we can cook on the grill outside."

"I can handle that," he said confidently. "*And* the outside bathroom. *And* the hand pump at the well. But I will miss taking a shower with you," he teased.

"There's an old copper tub in the shed that we might both be able to fit into. But you'd have to get a fire going in the stove, heat the water in pots, fill the tub—"

"I'll wait until we get back to civilization," he decided, even though his arms and shoulders were killing him and a good hot bath would have been a godsend. He massaged his shoulder, trying to work out the cramp, due, he assumed, to pushing brooms and mops all day. How was it, he wondered, that he could play tennis for hours and never feel a pang?

Andi, of course, noticed. "Muscles aching?"

"No, babe. I feel great. Ready for my next task. I got an A on housecleaning, right?"

"A plus," she decided. "The points are adding up. But there's another big chore ahead."

He moaned and followed her onto the porch.

"I noticed a couple of heavy branches had fallen onto the roof. They probably broke off in the last bad storm. We need to get them down and check the shingles to make sure the limbs haven't done any damage."

Sean moved past her into the yard. "What is this *we*, babe? Roof repair is a guy kind of thing."

"Maybe in your world, but here on Pawlie's, it's always been a girl job. Pam and I used to climb around on the roof like squirrels, cleaning out the gutters, tacking down loose shingles. You know, I'm not some kind of porcelain doll—"

"No argument there."

"So if you'll help me with the ladder, I'll go up."

"Nope. I'll get the ladder and I'll climb it. I'm on an A-plus roll and don't want to stop the momentum."

It wasn't the light aluminum extension ladder he expected. "What the hell is this?" he asked as he tried to drag it out of the shed.

"Need a little help?" She grabbed one end and together they pulled it free. "Dad made the ladder out of two-by-four pine planks. It's very sturdy."

Sean didn't disagree. It was also about a mile long and heavy as lead, but with Andi's help he dragged it up the path and leaned it against the house. Then with a show of bravado, he climbed up and stepped onto the roof.

He hadn't mentioned that he really didn't like heights. He didn't fear them, exactly, he told himself. Just wasn't fond of them. He would have preferred to remain on solid ground, holding the ladder for her as she'd done for him—and giving the orders.

"Check the big one first. It may have to be sawed in half," she yelled at him.

"Like this is brain surgery?" he mumbled under his breath as he struggled to get his footing on the slippery roof. It was steeper than it looked from the ground, and he had to crouch to keep his balance, which did nothing for the cool take-charge image he was trying to project.

Undaunted, he moved toward the peak of the roof where a limb was lodged against the chimney. It looked more like a tree trunk than a branch, and lifting it proved to be difficult. But he was damned if he'd climb down to get a saw and spend what was left of the day hacking at branches. After a long struggle, he moved around to the other side of the chimney, braced his foot against it and managed to work the branch free.

"Got it," he called out triumphantly. "Stay where you are, Andi. I'm going to throw it over this side—into the backyard."

"Are you sure you can manage?" she called out.

"Not a problem," he assured her as he lifted the heavy branch to chest level. "Look out below!" He summoned all his strength and hurled it into the air.

The branch sailed over the edge of the roof—and so did Sean.

He'd felt his feet fly out from under him and tried to grab the chimney. But he missed and hit the roof with a thud, and then like a human toboggan slid on his backside along the shingles.

Just as his legs shot over the edge, he managed to turn and catch hold of the gutter, where he hung, swaying like a flag, in midair.

"Andi!" he called.

"Where are you?"

"Get the ladder!" he yelled.

"What? I can't hear you."

"Get the— Oh, never mind." The gutter came loose from the house, bent and broke with a loud metallic crack.

She'll hear that, Sean thought as he crashed toward the ground, still holding onto the broken gutter.

"Sean?" She rounded the corner of the house in time to see him flying through the air. "Oh, no!" She ran toward him, her imagination working overtime. What if he broke his arm—his leg—his neck! What if— She visualized him in a hospital bed, on his back, in traction.

With a loud thud, Sean landed right on his derriere.

He was shocked, surprised—but not hurt. Relief flowed through her. She realized her legs were shaky. Thank God he was all right.

She sank onto the ground beside him. "You're all right," she said with relief. Then she began to laugh. "Oh, honey, if you could have seen the look on your face when you landed."

"I'm sure it was very amusing."

She realized he wasn't happy and knew she should offer sympathy, but it was too late. She couldn't stop laughing.

Breathing heavily, Sean sank into the bed of pine needles, which had softened the impact of his fall. "I'm glad you find this all so funny. Andi, do you realize that I could have broken my damned leg?"

"Of course I know that. But you didn't." Andi fought in vain to stifle her laughter.

"What's so amusing about that?" His face was tight, his lips clenched.

"Sorry, darling. But if you could have seen... It was so..."

"You're just speechless, right?" Sean got to his feet. "Well, I'm hot and tired, and right now I'd like a shower." He headed toward the front of the house. "Unfortunately, there's no such thing on this little family island."

"Oh, but there is."

He stopped in midstride. "I thought—"

"Well, there's no hot water, but there is a shower."

"I'm not in the mood for games, Andi."

She stood beside him. "This isn't a game, and there is a shower. The water's not hot, but it's wet."

He looked at her, silent and glowering.

"The shower's beyond the toolshed. There's a tank above that fills with rainwater. Just pull the handle and it'll shower down on you."

"Sounds great," Sean said between gritted teeth.

Andi watched with a frown as he stalked off. She knew she shouldn't have laughed. It was rude and thoughtless, but the sight of the glamorous Sean Fleming, clinging to a swaying gutter and then falling on his rear in a bed of pine needles, had been priceless. It had also been ludicrous and ridiculous, and in some strange way very endearing.

Now he was suffering from a bad case of ego damage, but that would pass. And she would make it up to him. Tonight. Her eyes strayed to the second floor of the house. In their bedroom, the big soft double bed was waiting.

BY TWILIGHT, Sean had recovered his equilibrium. The sun was heading toward an azure ocean. He paused long enough to appreciate the sight. Then he picked up the blanket, basket of food and cooler. They'd decided to have a dinner picnic at the beach, and he was in charge.

"Let me do something to help," Andi offered.

"Grab a pillow, babe. The man of the house is totally in charge."

When they got to the beach, he settled her on the blanket and poured two glasses of white wine, which had cooled to the perfect temperature on the ice. Andi looked fabulous. Her skin had a golden glow from the boat ride and a day in the sun. Her brown hair glistened; her dark eyes were wide and sparkling. And he couldn't fault her choice of clothing. Her trim, taut body was packed into yellow shorts and T-shirt. She was a sunbeam in the night.

He felt pretty good himself, refreshed after his shower, which was cold, God knows, but invigorating. Dressed in khaki shorts and a polo shirt, he sipped his wine, a great Chardonnay, he had to admit. He watched the sun on its colorful way to the horizon, leaving streaks of orange, peach and lavender across the sky. The humidity didn't thrill him, but a slight breeze had come up to cool things off a little. Perfection was very close. A beach. A sunset. The woman he loved. Everything was on track, and as long as he stayed off the roof, this could work.

He raised his glass in salute. "Here's to us."

Andi smiled and took a sip of wine. "It's great."

He nodded in response to the tribute.

"I don't want to bring up a sore subject, but I need to apologize for this afternoon—"

He interrupted. "No, don't apologize. It didn't seem very funny to me at the time—obviously—but I can see the humor now." He gazed at her intently. "That's why we're good together, Andi. You don't let me take myself too seriously. In TV land, I'm surrounded by yes people. Sometimes I lose perspective."

She grinned impishly. "Let's just say I keep you grounded."

He laughed and asked, "So how'd I do as a handyman?"

Andi leaned back on her pillow, sipping her wine. "Well, you certainly get A for effort. You tried hard enough. But for style and execution—"

"Don't tell me I failed just because of a slight accident beyond my control?"

"Well . . ." She drew the word out slowly, pretending to be thoughtful as she looked over the darkening sky and sea. "No, not a failure," she decided. "But maybe a D. A low, low D."

"Wait a minute," he cautioned. "You've forgotten about that huge branch, which I managed to get off the roof, saving your house from total disaster, I'm sure."

She laughed. "So I did. Let's call it a D plus."

"Not a C minus? Even if I get rid of the other branch tomorrow?" He thought about climbing onto the roof again, grimaced, but didn't back down.

"Hmm." She was thoughtful.

"I'll wait until you have a taste of tonight's dinner before pressing the issue," he said with a smile.

"So far, you're doing pretty well in the food department." She paused briefly. "Except for that breakfast."

"So you didn't like the soggy cereal? Never fear. Tonight I'll blow everything off the charts. And then tomorrow . . ."

"We enter a whole new arena tomorrow, Sean," she warned. "Just the two of us, on our own with no interference from anyone."

He leaned over and kissed her. "Nothing could be better."

She slipped her arms around his waist. "I hope so. Now about this idea. You grade me to make the test fair and equal."

"But you're perfect already."

"Oh, no, I'm not. What about when you fell off the roof—"

"And you laughed," he finished.

"Or when you first got to Clarion and I wanted to throw you out of the house?"

"Now that you mention it, sometimes you are less than angelic. Let's say you get an A for cleaning and an F for laughing at me."

She giggled happily and settled against his chest. "The night is so perfect, I'd like to stay here forever, just like this."

"Me, too, but we have to sit up long enough to eat."

"Later. For now let's watch the sunset."

AN HOUR and two glasses of wine later, Sean set out dinner with Andi exclaiming as he pulled each dish from the basket. "I don't believe it, goose liver pâté!"

"To remind us of that weekend in Provence."

"And calamari salad—"

"Mykonos. Remember the hotel overlooking the harbor?" he asked.

"Oh, I remember." She opened a carton of pasta with a rich white vegetable sauce. "Primivera. Northern Italy..."

"Venice, to be exact. Remember the little place on the Grand Canal?"

"Mmm." Did she ever. That had been one of their most romantic evenings. She opened a box of sweets from Vienna, which he had presented to her like a trophy. "Fabulous. But pretty soon, I guess, it'll be baked beans and beef jerky."

Sean didn't answer. He simply smiled.

They finished dinner as a squadron of mosquitoes burst out of the brush, causing them to pack up the gear fast and flee to the house.

Andi lit a couple of citronella candles while Sean poured a tumbler of brandy for her. "Not as good as your dad's . . ."

But it was equally comforting as it slid warmly down her throat, relaxing her totally. She closed her eyes, took a deep breath and sighed lazily. Suddenly she was very tired. Her bones felt heavy, and she stifled a yawn. "Let's get the dishes put away."

"My job. You go upstairs, turn down the bed, light the candles—" He kissed her lingeringly, and she returned his kiss, a brandied kiss filled with salt air and sunshine.

"I won't be long," he promised.

Andi climbed the stairs in a dreamy haze and all but floated into the bedroom. By candlelight, their bed looked incredibly inviting with soft, fluffy pillows, crisp white sheets and a colorful spread across the foot. She peeled out of her clothes and slipped into a white cotton nightgown. Lying down on the bed, she took a deep breath, more relaxed than she'd felt in months. She closed her eyes and inhaled the scents and sounds of the night, the saltiness of the breeze, the fragrance of lavender on the sheets, the call of crickets and the murmur of wind in the pines. Far away, she barely heard the gentle splash of waves against the rocky shore.

A few minutes later, Sean came into the room, whistling happily. Dishes done, kitchen clean, he was in a great mood, a mood for Andi.

She was already in bed, stretched out on one side with her back to the door. "Andi..." He moved around the bed. Her eyes were closed, her lashes soft brown fans against her cheeks. Her hair was a dark shadow across the pillow. She was sound asleep.

He could wake her, but he wasn't going to. They had two weeks to make love—once a day, twice a day, all day. He smiled. One night wouldn't make any difference.

5

ANDI ROLLED OVER and sat up in bed at the first rays of morning sun. Sean still slept soundly, sprawled across most of the bed, his bare chest glistening golden in the light. She remained quiet for a while beside him, watching his peaceful slumber. Damn, he was something, with his tawny hair tousled across his forehead and his two-day growth of beard. That was currently the style, but Sean was a style setter, not a follower, and she expected he'd either shave soon or start a beard. At the moment, though, he looked very handsome.

She thought about kissing him awake and then decided against it. He looked so contented. Besides, he'd let her sleep off her exhaustion last night. It was only fair to do the same for him this morning. The smell of coffee would wake him soon enough.

She grabbed her clothes and shoes and slipped out of the bedroom, unable to resist one look back. It wasn't difficult to understand why she'd fallen for Sean Fleming or why she was so determined to work things out.

Sean had left a packet of gourmet coffee on the counter. "He does think of everything," she said aloud. Of course, he was also taking no chance that she might come up with an inferior brand or, heaven forbid, a jar of instant.

It didn't take long to fill the old wood-burning stove with kindling, start a fire and draw a bucket of water from the well. While the coffee brewed, she went out on the front porch and took a long, satisfying breath of cool, clean air. Through the pines she could glimpse the bay sparkling in the light. This was the most beautiful time of day, she thought, early morning when the world was fresh and new. All she needed now was her husband beside her, sharing it with her.

Oh, well, there would be lots of other mornings, and she was determined they would be different from the ones they'd shared in the past. In fact, they hadn't really *ever* shared a morning. On stolen weekends when they lived abroad, they'd stayed up late, made love half the night, then wakened at noon, only to make love again.

She smiled ruefully. The lovemaking would only get better. But the rest was going to change—starting now. As soon as the scent of coffee brewing reached his nostrils, Sean would be up to enjoy this wonderful morning with her.

TWO HOURS and several cups of coffee later, she was on the porch, binoculars on her lap, studying a bird identification book. Usually avid about bird-watching, Andi had gotten bored quickly and was routinely turning the pages as birds flew by unnoticed.

Sean finally appeared, dressed in a pair of cotton shorts, barefooted, his hair still tousled. She noticed all that out of the corner of her eye but didn't look up.

He crossed the porch and dropped a kiss on her hair. "Morning, babe."

"Good morning," she answered a little stiffly.

"So, what's for breakfast?"

"I was waiting for you," she replied.

That's when he noticed the tone of her voice. "Uh-oh. Did we have a date for breakfast?"

"No," she admitted, "but I had the fantasy that we'd share our first breakfast out here on the porch just as the sun came up."

He checked out the sky. "Guess I missed that by a little while."

She managed a smile. "Well, you worked hard yesterday."

He sat down beside her and pulled on his running shoes. "So did you."

"But you didn't get to sleep until later last night. It'll be different tomorrow when we get a schedule worked out," she said, putting aside the book.

"Schedule?" He looked at her. "Is that part of our test?"

"It's called being in sync," she answered. "Which is a large part of what this experiment is all about."

Sean nodded as he laced up his shoes. So having breakfast together at dawn was important to her. He hadn't known that before. "Okay, starting tomorrow, we'll have breakfast together. But for now I'm going on my run."

"When did you become a runner?"

He stood and braced himself against the porch railing. "About the time you left me," he said over his shoulder as he stretched first one leg and then the other. "I needed something to work off my restless energy."

"I didn't know," she said.

"And I didn't know you were a birder. Maybe *that's* what this experiment is all about, Andi. Learning what we don't know."

"Maybe," she said thoughtfully. Maybe this wasn't going to go exactly as she planned, either.

"Back soon, babe." He gave her a quick kiss and was gone.

Andi watched him break into a run and head down the path toward the bay. So far, her morning had been less than satisfactory, but the day was still young. Besides, he'd been right when he said this trip was more than a test. It was a learning experience.

She knew a little more about him already, Andi thought as she went into the kitchen, all set to put together a great breakfast for them to share when he got back from his run.

But as she began to look through the cartons she learned something else about him that didn't please her at all.

"More pâté?" She pushed aside a stack of cans and pulled out half a dozen jars of caviar. Puzzled, she opened another box, only to find more of the same— gourmet foods, beautifully packaged. Where were the staples of a camping trip, the cans of beans, stewed tomatoes and the rest? Not here!

As she pulled out more and more containers, her puzzlement turned to amazement. Gourmet food. Tons of it. Canned salmon and Greek peppers. Shortbread from Scotland and cookies from Vienna. An epicurean's delight, but worthless for putting together healthy meals during two weeks in the woods.

She could find nothing that would make an edible breakfast. No eggs, no pancake mix, not one box of cereal. What had Sean been thinking?

She did the best she could with leftovers, slathering cheese over the remainder of last night's loaf of French bread. She stuck it in the heated oven and waited for Sean to return.

Another hour passed. Waiting wasn't such a big deal for Andi. She'd done a lot of it during their marriage. That would have to change. But first things first—the food problem.

Finally, breathing heavily, his face flushed and hair damp, Sean strolled into the kitchen.

"Good run?" Andi rummaged in a duffel bag and tossed him a towel.

"Great," he replied, wiping his face and neck. "You're right about the island. It's pretty wild and unspoiled. I'm ready to see more, if you'll give me the royal tour." He gave her a big hug. "But for now, I'm monstrously hungry, wife."

"Breakfast is in the oven," she answered. "Cheese toast."

"That's different," he commented, "but just so there's lots of it."

"Oh, there's lots, all right. Lots of caviar. Champagne. Anchovies and olives and chutney. Does that sound like breakfast food, Sean?"

"Depends on where you're breakfasting," he said absently, giving her a kiss.

"How about on a primitive island in the middle of the bay? When you went shopping for this trip, did you think we'd be eating caviar for breakfast? Where are the staples?" she asked without giving him a chance to respond.

"Staples?" He poured a cup of coffee.

"You know what they are, don't you? Flour, sugar, powdered milk—"

"Oh, those. I thought you'd have all that stuff here. In the pantry."

"We have nothing in the pantry. In fact, we don't even have a pantry," she said. "We haven't been here in ages. I thought I told you that."

"You didn't tell me there was *nothing* here." He shrugged and grinned. "It's not like we could run out to the store . . ."

She saw the teasing in his eyes but kept a straight face. "Unless you're a champion swimmer. You know where Clarion is." She pointed toward the bay. "About fifteen miles that way."

"And no neighbors to borrow from . . ."

She rolled her eyes. "Not unless you count the local chipmunks." She paused. "We could always steal their food supply. I guess you could call nuts a kind of staple."

He saw the trace of a smile beginning on her lips and gave her another little kiss. "You're keeping your sense of humor, I'm glad to see."

"What else can I do?" she said with a shrug.

"I'm in trouble," he decided. "But I challenge the bad rating you're about to give me."

"I haven't decided how to grade this—" she indicated the boxes "—this gourmet mountain."

Sean laughed again. "Before you decide, let me plead my case. I'm innocent based on ignorance."

It was Andi's turn to laugh.

"I'm not talking about my IQ," he said quickly. "I was ignorant of the lack of staples here."

"I'll take that under consideration," she said.

"Good. Then I'll do the same for you."

She looked at him with a frown.

"I won't fault you for burning the toast."

"Oh, no!" She pushed past Sean, grabbed a hot pad and rescued the toast from the oven.

"Barely singed," Sean said, breaking off a piece. "Oh, but hot!" He dropped the toast onto the floor.

"Good thing we just mopped up, because you're going to have to eat that. It's the total breakfast."

He picked up the toast, blew it off and took a bite. "I'm adaptable."

"But tell me, darling, what are we going to live on for the next two weeks? Pâté and caviar?"

"Why not?" He held out his cup, and she poured him some coffee. "Or we can live on love."

She sighed. "You're impossible."

He gave her a toasty kiss. "Impossibly good or impossibly bad?"

"Some of both."

He hugged her and lifted her feet from the floor. "So you're not angry anymore?"

"I wasn't angry this morning, just lonely. Think about it, Sean. I spent the entire morning waiting for you." She slid down his body to the floor, but he didn't let go. "Let's make a vow to do things differently from now on. Together—as a team. Isn't that the test for both of us? How well we work as a team?"

"Sure. Cook together . . ."

"And run together . . ."

"Don't tell me you're a runner?"

"I can trot along behind you."

"Okay, starting now, we'll be a team. Together twenty-four hours a day, never a moment apart—"

"Hold everything!" She laughed. "I'm not suggesting that. We both get our space—whenever we want it."

"But when we're together, we're really together."

"Like last night?" she asked with a grin.

"That was an exception. Our body clocks were set differently. They were still out of sync this morning, but we're on the same time now. Tomorrow morning I'll wake up at dawn—"

She laughed. "You're going too far again, Sean. Let's compromise. I'll sleep a little later, you get up a little earlier."

"You got a deal. Now about the together part . . ." He swept her into his arms and carried her into the big room, where they settled in one of the overstuffed chairs.

"*This* is what I call together." He kissed her slowly, thoroughly. Her lips were sweet on his, and her body was warm and yielding. Desire built in him, hot and heavy. "What are the plans for today?" he murmured.

He felt her breath, rapid and shallow against his cheek, heard her heart thumping against his chest. "I thought we might take the day off—explore, swim, go for a ride in the canoe . . ."

He nuzzled the soft skin of her neck and ran his tongue along its satiny smoothness. He heard her sigh, felt her tremble in his arms, which he wrapped more tightly around her. "But first," he whispered, "we have unfinished business from last night."

"Oh, I think it's more pleasure than business," she replied.

"You're so right," he said, "and the pleasure starts now."

SEAN DOWNED a cool glass of water from the well. It was clean and sweet and almost as good as a cold beer, the perfect refreshment at the end of a great day.

It had started with their incredible lovemaking and segued into an exploration of the island, from the beaches on the west side to the cliffs on the east, where the sea pounded dramatically against the rocks. They walked through the pine forests to a surprising sunlit meadow, swam in the cold, bracing azure waters of the bay and made love on a strip of sandy beach between the rocky precipices. Andi called it her secret place, and she'd never shared it with anyone until now.

Just before sunset, they'd returned to the cabin, tired, thirsty and hungry.

He poured a glass of water and took it to Andi, who sat at the long wooden table in the big room. Her hoard of seashells, collected on their walk, was spread out before her. She held up one for him to admire.

"So, you're a birder *and* a shell collector."

"Outdoor hobbies for an outdoor girl," she commented as she continued to separate the shells.

Sean sat beside her. "Funny that I've never thought of you that way."

"Why not? My folks ran an outfitting business, so it figures."

"I guess so. Maybe I just never saw you in the outdoor setting."

"Not much opportunity in Paris or Rome. That's why we're here, Sean. To get to know each other without all the—"

"Yep, without all the trappings of civilization. Speaking of the real world, where's the radio you told me about?" he asked casually.

"Planning to tune in to the news? I didn't think you'd be able to stay away from your job."

"I haven't given the outside world a thought. How could I with such a wonderful diversion?" he added, putting his arm around her.

"Then why do you want the radio?"

"Simple. We need to know it's in working order in case of emergency." He grinned. "Or maybe to contact the mainland for a special delivery of cold beer and canned beans."

"The radio is in the closet. And you don't fool me for a minute." She got up. "I'm going to take a shower."

"I'll come with you."

Andi held up her hand to stop him. "Nope. If you recall, it's a one-person shower."

"What about togetherness?"

"Save that for when I get back. We'll work on dinner—together."

Sean headed for the closet to search out the radio. "Whatever you say, babe."

He didn't recognize it at first, the thing was so ancient. He pulled it out, blew off the dust and put it on the table. He was reminded of shortwave radios he'd seen in old movies. But it didn't look too complicated. With luck, he would be able to operate it.

He pushed the on switch, turned up the volume and whirled the dial. Nothing happened. He gave the thing a bang with the palm of his hand. Nothing. What the hell was the matter? Then it hit him. They'd probably brought the blasted thing over here years ago. Of course, there was no power because the batteries were dead.

In the closet, he found extra batteries carefully sealed against the damp. As soon as he replaced them, the radio came to life with the welcoming crackle of static. Sean smiled. Nothing to it. He turned up the volume and twirled the dial, sliding past a weather update and fisherman's advisory and stopping on the world news report, scratchy, a little tinny, but very welcome.

"Today in the Middle East, warring factions agreed to . . ."

Sean smiled in satisfaction. The real world at last. But it would have to wait a while longer. He heard Andi's footsteps on the porch. Quickly, he turned off the radio and put it under the table.

She appeared in the doorway, fresh from her shower, hair still damp. "Ready for some togetherness in the kitchen?"

"I've been thinking of nothing else," he said with a satisfied smirk as he met her at the door and accompanied her to the kitchen.

She turned to him. "So this is it. The two of us in the kitchen together for the first time. What's for dinner?"

"I have an idea. I'll close my eyes, reach into one of the boxes and pull something out. Then we'll—"

"Sean," she interrupted, "I'm being serious. If we were talking about a little snack, I'd be happy to play your games. But I'm hungry. Starving, actually, and I'd like a solid meal." She rooted through one of the boxes. "Sun-dried tomatoes, olives . . . Maybe we could do something Mediterranean. I think we have a cookbook that—"

Sean stopped her. "Recipes? Are you a coward, woman? We're two people with great taste and fabulous imaginations. Between us, we can come up with something incredible."

"Something we agree on?" she asked.

"Damn right. We're a team, remember."

She nodded. "Except that one of the team members is a little less adventurous than the other."

He leaned over and nuzzled her neck. "Oh, yeah? I never would have known that—from your spirit of adventure this morning in the chair."

"Well—"

"I believe you're blushing, Andi."

"No, I'm not," she denied. "But we're in the kitchen now, not in the . . . chair."

"Or on the beach...or in bed." He stopped. "Come to think of it, we haven't made love in the bed upstairs yet, have we?"

"Sean, stop it. We're talking about dinner."

"All right," he said. "Everything in its proper place. From now on, we only make love in bed."

"Well, let's not go that far," she said with a big smile. "Now, about dinner."

He checked out the boxes and came up with a few items that he declared interesting. "Aha. Capers. Just what we need. Here's a bottle of Italian olive oil—virgin, of course," he added wickedly. "Canned clams, coconut—"

"You brought coconut but not rice and beans?"

"Who needs necessities when you can have luxuries?" He juggled the coconut from hand to hand. "Sorry this is shredded and packaged, but there are not a lot of palm trees in Bangor, Maine. Hey, I remember buying canned shrimp. There's a great Tahitian dish with shrimp and coconut—"

"I definitely don't have any recipes for Tahitian dishes," she told him.

"Trust me, Andi, I can duplicate the dish without a recipe."

"What about proportions?"

"No problem. I'll never forget that little restaurant in Papeete, right on the harbor." A faraway look came into his eyes.

"You may remember the restaurant, but I bet you never knew the recipe. Someone else was doing the cooking that night, right? Now, what about a simple dinner of pasta and clam sauce?"

"No way. I'm thinking of something exotic like bouillabaisse or paella," he countered.

"Sean, we don't have the ingredients."

"So we substitute. Live a little, babe."

Andi realized he wasn't going to listen to reason. She was defeated.

"Now, if you'll just find the can opener and hand me a bowl—"

She put her hands on her hips. "Is that what you call working together—you give the orders and I do the fetching?"

"Of course not, but let's face it, you know where all the utensils are. I don't."

She sighed. Sean was right—and she was right. He definitely saw himself as head chef, with her as sous-chef, she realized as she pulled out bowls, spatulas, knives and pots.

"I think definitely bouillabaisse," he said, opening the cans of crab and shrimp.

"Doesn't bouillabaisse have fish heads in it?"

"Purist," he scoffed.

"Maybe we should save this dish for tomorrow. We might even be able to catch a couple of fish," she volunteered. "I'm sure there's fishing gear around here somewhere."

"We'll save that for another dinner. I'm in the mood for bouillabaisse *tonight*," he decided. "Remember the great little hotel in Nice? I'm pretty sure we had bouillabaisse there."

"We did. With fish heads," she added.

Sean was paying no attention. "I need some tomatoes, babe."

"We only have sun-dried." She held up a large jar.

"Then toss 'em in."

"Sean, that won't work." She looked with dismay at the conglomeration he was mixing in a large frying pan.

"Support and cooperation, that's what I'm looking for, babe. Now are you with me or against me?"

"I'm not sure. I'm beginning to wonder if this kitchen is big enough for both of us." Sean had covered every surface with empty cans and jars, adding utensils, mixing bowls and measuring cups with abandon as he used them and tossed them aside.

"The measuring cups are actually for measuring, Sean," she reminded him. "I'm afraid you're going to get an F for organization."

"You're not doing so great in the helper department," he shot back. "And as for the measuring cups, to me they're just containers. Measuring is for sissies," he declared confidently. "Now, chop me some garlic, babe. We're going to need lots of spices."

Andi said nothing as she cleared a space on the counter for her cutting board, thinking the more spices the better, to cover the flavor of whatever Sean was creating.

Blithely, he went on adding ingredients, tossing them in his pan with abandon, having a wonderful time.

"Not the capers!" she warned as he opened the bottle.

"Too late," he said. "They're going to add something special."

Andi gritted her teeth. It was only dinner, she told herself, but from now on, they'd take turns cooking. That may not be togetherness, but it was a kind of sharing, the only kind possible, since she couldn't bear to watch what Sean did to a meal.

ANDI SCOURED the dishes, pots and pans and rinsed them in cold water, after hustling Sean into the other room. It had been tough enough to cook in the same kitchen with him, and she knew cleaning up together would be impossible. They'd be stepping all over each other, and the little irritations felt earlier might explode into something more serious. She wasn't going to chance that.

Tomorrow Sean could heat the water and finish washing up. She'd done the hard part, which she figured balanced the fact that he'd done most of the cooking, such as it was.

"You're awfully quiet," he yelled out. "Did the meal leave you speechless?"

"More or less. I guess it was the combination of flavors. I can truly say I've never tasted anything like it."

Andi tightened the tie around the plastic garbage bag, where she'd dumped the remainder of her dinner. What could she say to Sean? He'd given the meal his all, but it was obvious that he was the world's worst cook. She doubted if he'd argue about that, considering he left most of his dinner on the plate, too.

"What're you doing?" she called.

"Building a fire for us to sit in front of while we neck and drink brandy. Mostly neck," he added.

Andi didn't mention that they'd had enough heat in the kitchen—and not just from the wood-burning stove! If Sean wanted a fire, he'd have a fire; she wasn't going to argue about it.

She stepped onto the back porch to cool off before facing more heat. She needed to put everything in perspective so there'd be no more near-arguments. One thing was for sure, if this marriage test was going to work, there'd have to be lots of give and take.

She leaned against the porch rail. Dinner had been a failure and had left a bad taste in her mouth—in more ways than one. But Andi was aware that all marriages went through a period of adjustment at one time or another. Better in the kitchen than some other room of the house, she thought wryly.

They could easily get past culinary problems. They'd already decided that togetherness wasn't always the answer, and she was pretty sure Sean would agree with dividing the kitchen chores. One problem solved, she decided as she went inside and headed into the big room. What they needed now was a little snuggle by the fire.

She found him crouched on the hearth.

"There're some newspapers on the back porch," she suggested, noticing that he was having trouble firing up the kindling.

"Don't need 'em," he answered.

Andi forced herself to shut up and sit down. Building fires had been one of her jobs when the family came to the cabin, and she knew all the eccentricities of the fireplace. First the paper, then the kindling, then the logs. Sean had skipped the first step. She'd tried to advise him. He'd chosen not to listen.

"Toss me some matches, babe?" he asked.

"The fireplace draws a little weirdly," she warned. "Be sure the flue is open. The lever is on the right-hand side—"

"I've already opened it."

"Are you sure? If you look up there, you can see the sky when it's open."

Sean turned toward her. "I'm not going to stick my head up the chimney. The flue's open, Andi."

Sean struck a match and touched it to the kindling. It blazed for a moment, and he turned toward Andi with a self-satisfied smirk. Then it went out. Andi bit her lip and kept quiet while he lit another match.

This time the kindling caught fire, crackling as the tiny flames licked at it.

Sean stood up. "Nothing to it," he said, adding larger twigs and branches.

Andi drew a breath of relief before realizing that it was a smoky breath. In fact, smoke was billowing all around. "The flue—open the flue," she shouted.

"I told you, I already opened it," Sean answered. "That's probably just a little backup. Happens when you light a fire for the first time in a while. I used to do this for my mother all the time, and I know . . ."

He was stopped by the smoke, which now filled the room.

Andi, choking, gasped for breath. "It's still closed!" She ran past him and reached for the lever, pushing it to one side. Acrid smoke filled her nose and eyes. "*Now* it's open."

They retreated to the front porch. The smell of smoke clung to her skin, hair and clothes. "Someone must have left the flue open and then you closed it," she said to Sean.

Defensive and disheveled, he wasn't a very convincing presence. "I can't be responsible for what other people do."

Andi was feeling pretty defensive herself. "Well, what was I supposed to do, check it out for you?"

"Yeah," he decided.

"You wouldn't even let me give you advice about—" Suddenly she broke off in mid-sentence, went over to Sean and put her arms around him. "I can't believe we're arguing about a fireplace flue!"

Sean laughed. "It does seem pretty silly, but it's part of the test—on which I get an F, huh?"

"Unavoidable," she said. "But you're right, I should have checked it out, so there's no passing grade for me, either."

"That's pretty big of you, babe."

She laughed and gave him a smoky kiss. "Let's forget the fire, and dinner—"

"Let's definitely forget dinner," he quipped. "From now on, no meals without a recipe."

"And from now on, I'll keep out of your way. In fact, I was thinking that a good compromise would be to alternate cooking chores. One night I'll cook for you—"

"And the next night I'm the chef, complete with cookbook," he added quickly. "Great idea."

Andi hugged him tightly. Despite their missteps, the day had been fun, and miraculously they were still speaking. Even laughing. They might not be much of a team yet, but they were trying, and that counted for a lot.

"While the smoke clears, what about a canoe ride? Pawlie's Island by moonlight."

Andi took his hand. "Perfect ending to a perfect day."

6

"THIS IS THE LIFE," Andi said over her shoulder as she paddled.

Launching the old canoe had been surprisingly easy, and almost at once she and Sean had established a fluid, rhythmic pattern, matching each other stroke for stroke. They crested the slight rise of waves and headed into the deeper water of the bay with Andi in the bow and Sean in the stern. "I can't believe the perfect rhythm we've got going."

"So we're a great team, after all," Sean commented. "I knew it. Harmonious," he added.

"Well, in this one area at least," Andi noted.

"Now that we've proven how well our partnership works, isn't it time for a rest?"

"Let's keep going a little longer. It's great exercise," Andi suggested.

"Exercise! Andi, get real. I ran for an hour this morning, we hiked the island, and our lovemaking—you know how many calories that burns. What we don't need is more exercise."

"Just a little farther," she insisted as the canoe skimmed along. "When we get to deep water, it'll be calm and we can relax and float."

Finally, ten minutes later, Andi put down her paddle and Sean did the same. "Now," he said, "*this* is the life. Turn around, Andi, and look. It's moon glow."

Light from the full moon spilled across the water, bathing them with its silvery sheen. The night was soft, serene and cloudless, with thousands of stars gleaming overhead.

Andi carefully turned on the seat to face Sean. "It's heavenly," she said, musing as she let her hand drift through the water. "I never would have dreamed this scenario. Me and Sean Fleming floating in a canoe off a tiny island in Penobscot Bay."

"And I certainly didn't imagine this kind of thing when we met in Switzerland."

"Life is always full of surprises—like your being a great canoeist."

"That's part of learning about each other, babe. Would you believe that I went to summer camp a couple of times when I was a kid?"

"Never," she responded.

"Yep. Sean, the Boy Scout. Didn't enjoy it much," he admitted.

"Were there girls at your camp?"

He shook his head and laughed. "I imagine that was the problem. If you'd been there in your little Girl Scout uniform, it would have been different. You *were* a Girl Scout, weren't you, Andi?"

She nodded.

"How come that doesn't surprise me? Little Andi traipsing through the woods with her trusty hatchet. Or organizing the girls for a boating trip. You're good at that. But there's one thing missing on *this* outing. You know what it is, don't you?"

"Wine? Or maybe food? A picnic?" Andi realized she was still hungry.

"Get real, babe. What we need is love, romance—amour. You should be here with me, cuddling in the moonlight, kissing... Wait, I have an even better idea. Have you ever done it in a canoe?" he asked in a low, tantalizing voice.

"*It?*" she teased. "What in the world do you mean?"

"I'll show you." He started to get up, and the boat rocked dangerously.

"Don't stand up," she warned.

He stood up.

"Don't try to walk in the boat."

He began to walk. "Too late. I'm on my way."

"Sean, we'll capsize," she cautioned.

"No, we won't. We're old scouts, remember? If the canoe tilts toward the port side, lean starboard. Nothing to it."

He started toward her.

"Careful!" she cried immediately as they dipped toward the starboard side. "Port," she called out. "Lean!"

Then she leaned, and realized too late that was a big mistake.

The canoe rolled onto its side, tossing them into the icy waters of Penobscot Bay.

She sputtered to the surface. Sean's head bobbed beside her.

"Why the hell did you tell me to lean?" he asked, spitting a stream of water.

"Those were your instructions," she shot back.

"I told *you* to—"

"Then why the *hell*," she said, mocking him, "did you listen to me?"

"Never mind. This isn't the time to discuss it." The canoe had flipped upside down. "Hell, we'll never get the damned thing righted."

"You don't have to curse so much," she advised.

"How do you expect me to react, out here in the middle of the bay? Why did we have to paddle miles from shore?"

"Miles! We're no more than a couple of hundred yards."

"When we're swimming, those yards will seem like miles."

"I thought you were an old scout," she chided. Treading water, she pushed her wet hair from her face. It felt like wet seaweed plastered to her head.

"I was a hell of a lot younger then."

"There you go, cursing again."

"I need help, not moral instructions, Andi. Will you please find the paddles while I tow this damned— while I tow this canoe to shore?"

Without answering, Andi turned her back on him and splashed away.

THEY REACHED SHORE, and, soggy and silent, tied the canoe up and walked to the cabin.

"What we have here," Sean said as they climbed the porch stairs, "is a failure to communicate."

Andi didn't crack a smile at the old movie quote. It was too true to be amusing. So far, the only real communication she and Sean had experienced was while making love. That's how it had always been. Nothing had changed, and her marriage test was a bust.

"Maybe tomorrow will be better," she said wearily, as she pulled off her soaking shoes and socks and left them at the door. "Right now I'd like nothing more than a good hot bath—" Even as she spoke, Andi realized that was impossible. Neither she nor Sean had the energy to drag in the old copper tub, never mind draw water from the well and build a fire to heat it!

"Forget it," she said when he looked as if he was going to offer to make a bath possible for her. "I'm going to bed and wrap myself in a quilt."

As she headed up the stairs, Sean realized this second honeymoon, marriage test or whatever they called it, was a total mess. Why had he agreed to come to this godforsaken island? He stripped off his shirt and dropped it on the floor, thinking that right now they could be on the other side of the country, in San Francisco, maybe, having a fabulous dinner in an elegant hotel after exploring the romantic city.

But instead here they were, on an island with no plumbing, no hot water and no decent food. He took off his shoes and then peeled off his soaking pants. The food he'd brought was okay for an occasional picnic, but not for three meals a day. She was right about that. Tomorrow he'd get on the shortwave and ask Ed Ennis to ferry over some staples.

He grabbed an old afghan from the back of the sofa and wrapped it around his naked body. Then he poured himself a glass of brandy and drained it in one long swallow. Immediately, he felt warmer. It wasn't his idea of fun to go for an unexpected swim in the cold

AN IMPORTANT MESSAGE FROM THE EDITORS OF HARLEQUIN®

Dear Reader,

Because you've chosen to read one of our fine romance novels, we'd like to say "thank you"! And, as a **special** way to thank you, we've selected <u>four more</u> of the books you love so well, **and** a Cuddly Teddy Bear to send you absolutely *FREE!*

Please enjoy them with our compliments...

Editor,
Temptation

P.S. And because we value our customers, we've attached something extra inside ...

PEEL OFF SEAL AND PLACE INSIDE

HOW TO VALIDATE
YOUR
EDITOR'S FREE GIFT
"THANK YOU"

1. Peel off gift seal from front cover. Place it in space provided at right. This automatically entitles you to receive four free books and a Cuddly Teddy Bear.

2. Send back this card and you'll get brand-new Harlequin Temptation® novels. These books have a cover price of $3.50 each, but they are yours to keep absolutely free.

3. There's no catch. You're under no obligation to buy anything. We charge nothing — ZERO — for your first shipment. And you don't have to make any minimum number of purchases — not even one!

4. The fact is thousands of readers enjoy receiving books by mail from the Harlequin Reader Service®. They like the convenience of home delivery...they like getting the best new novels before they're available in stores...and they love our discount prices!

5. We hope that after receiving your free books you'll want to remain a subscriber. But the choice is yours — to continue or cancel, anytime at all! So why not take us up on our invitation, with no risk of any kind. You'll be glad you did!

6. Don't forget to detach your FREE BOOKMARK. And remember...just for validating your Editor's Free Gift Offer, we'll send you FIVE MORE gifts, *ABSOLUTELY FREE!*

GET A FREE TEDDY BEAR...
You'll love this plush, Cuddly Teddy Bear, an adorable accessory for your dressing table, bookcase or desk. Measuring 5½" tall, he's soft and brown and has a bright red ribbon around his neck — he's completely captivating! And he's yours absolutely free, when you accept this no-risk offer!

night water of the bay. He pulled the afghan closer around him. The damned bay was just about as icy as Andi's attitude when she marched up the stairs. He didn't blame her, actually. The dunking had pretty much cooled his amorous intentions, as well.

He poured another glass of brandy and nursed it and his irritation along. Hell, the food problem was part Andi's fault, too, he decided. He'd never been to Pawlie's Island. She could have told him there wasn't even a can of beans in the house. It was almost as if she'd been trying to set him up.

But he knew better than that. He might not know everything about Andi, her childhood, all her likes and dislikes, her hobbies, pastimes, favorite foods, things that—he supposed—husbands and wives knew about each other. But she loved him. Of that he was sure. Besides, she wasn't doing so damned great on the test, either.

And the situation certainly hadn't done anything for his language. As Andi noted, the cusses were pouring out, even in his thoughts. He figured it was time to behave with a little more sophistication.

He suddenly laughed out loud. This was sophistication? Standing here naked, wrapped in some little old lady's shawl?

So what was going on between him and Andi? He sank onto the chair where they'd made such delicious love, aware that the problem was just what he'd told her—and what she'd told him. Except for their love-making—where communication was right on—the two of them had a real problem, and they were going to have to make an effort to solve it.

Well, why not? They were reasonable, intelligent people, and more importantly, they were in love. There was no reason things couldn't work out. "Not a *damn* reason," he added as he got up and headed to bed where, no doubt, Andi would be sound asleep.

ANDI LACED her walking shoes and looked out over the bay. It was going to be another perfect day, cool, clear and cloudless.

"New day, clean slate," she said aloud. They'd both done miserably on the canoe outing. Sean should have known better than to stand up in a canoe, but she could imagine him as a show-off kid at camp doing just that—and getting applause for it. And she shouldn't have panicked when the canoe listed.

But all that was over and done. "Fs for both of us," she said.

"What?" Sean came out to the porch, looking sleepy, unfocused and still unshaven.

"Nothing," she replied quickly.

As he stretched his arms and squinted into the rising sun, she lifted her coffee cup in salute to a new day. "Good morning. Coffee's on."

He shook his head as if to clear the cobwebs. "Not for me. I'm ready for my run. What about you?"

"I'm almost ready, but I can't run on an empty stomach." He'd evidently forgotten that they were supposed to be meeting for breakfast. She decided not to mention it. There was a time to persist and a time to back off.

"That's the way you're supposed to do it, Andi. You don't eat before you run."

"I do," she said as she disappeared into the house.

Sean shrugged and began his stretching routine. He had no idea how the morning's run was going to turn out now that Andi had decided to join him. Running for him had never been a couple thing. It was a time to think, sort stuff out, get a clear head. Not something that could work in tandem. But he'd promised to share the morning with her, and he was going to keep that promise.

She came out nibbling on a cookie. "This was all I could find," she said defensively.

Should he wait for her to finish the cookie? he wondered. That seemed like the caring thing to do. So he tried to be patient, even though he was anxious to get going.

"Okay," she said finally, "let's do it."

"Which way?" he asked.

"Maybe along the beach?"

"Sounds good to me." He'd had his mind set on running through the pines to the meadow, but this was going to be a day of compromise, starting now.

Off they went down the path to the beach. He began at a slow, steady pace with Andi running along beside him.

"You're doing great, babe," he complimented.

"How far do you go?" Her question came in a little gasp.

"Three miles at least, usually four or five. Depends on the terrain."

Andi nodded. The tide was low, out beyond the rocks, and the sand was packed hard—optimum conditions, she thought, for running five miles. She should have suggested a tougher terrain and shortened the distance since, frankly, she was no runner. But she loved the beach at this time of morning. It was nature at its best, with clean air, clear water and so much life—urchins in the tide pools and at the water's edge and birds of every description, including a flock of sandpipers ahead of them. The birds fluttered away as they approached.

They laughed together in the wind as the sandpipers scattered. Sean was beginning to feel better. He filled his lungs with salt air. It was still cool, and promised to be a pleasant day, and he began to think that he could probably run forever. But could Andi? She'd kept pace okay so far, jogging just behind him. He decided to give her a little incentive by slowing so that she could pull ahead.

Just as he dropped back, Andi stopped suddenly, and he almost fell over her.

"Look at this, Sean," she exclaimed as he regained his balance. "It's a little army of crabs, marching along together."

This was what she considered a run, stopping after two hundred yards? He started to swear, bit his tongue and feigned interest for a minute, still pumping his legs. "Fascinating," he said, "but we need to keep moving."

"Oh, sorry. It's just that nature's out here in full force this time of morning."

To avoid offending Mother Nature, Sean didn't say anything as they got going again, this time at an increased pace. She would just have to keep up.

But the next time he looked around, she wasn't there. He slowed again, turned and saw her on her hands and knees in the sand between two large rocks. "Andi—"

She crouched lower, and he panicked for an instant and headed to her. "What's the matter, are you hurt—did you pull a muscle?"

She smiled at him. "Look at this tide pool, Sean. It's a wonderful microcosm of the sea. Crabs and minnows and little coquinas that burrow down in the sand. I remember early morning walks I used to take with my dad. We could spend hours just sitting and watching life in one of these little pools . . ."

Sean finally stopped her, speaking more sharply than he intended. "I'm not really interested in watching this microcosm of the sea, Andi. Maybe we can plan a nature stroll for another time, but right now I want to get my miles in."

Andi's eyes widened. "Then go right ahead and run. Don't let me hold you up. I guess I had the mistaken idea we were sharing the morning. I didn't know we were on some kind of schedule with no time to stop just to observe the life around us."

"Sorry for snapping," he replied. "I'm a little grouchy. Got to bed late . . ."

"That's hardly my fault," she retorted.

"I didn't say it was."

"But you implied—"

"No, I didn't—" Sean stopped short. "What're we doing arguing about this? We're supposed to be having fun, Andi. Together. And all that."

She just looked at him, as if waiting for more.

"All right. Let me look at these little...whatevers." He bent down, still pumping his legs to avoid cramping.

"Never mind. You've frightened them away."

"Sorry. But I have to keep moving—"

"Mmm." She was watching the pool intently.

"I guess if we stay here and wait awhile, they'll come back," he offered.

"I'll wait. You go run. That way, we'll both be happy."

Since neither of them was happy at the moment, Sean decided to take her advice. "Okay, I'll catch you on my way back," he said, keeping his voice as light and pleasant as possible.

He jogged off and then realized that he hadn't kissed her goodbye. Worse, he hadn't even kissed her good morning.

ANDI WATCHED HIM RETREAT. She'd seen a lot of that view recently, Sean going away. Admittedly, it was a great sight, his muscular back and legs, not to mention that great bottom. But considering what his constant departure was doing to them, she was getting pretty tired of the view.

For a long time, Andi sat quietly, thinking of nothing but the beauty of nature as she watched the sea creatures return. But after a while she got to her feet and walked slowly along the beach, letting herself face the problems in her marriage test. It wasn't the test itself. To be honest, Sean had passed it so far. Maybe he wasn't good at household chores, but he was trying, which was all she'd asked of him.

But the test had made clear that almost everything about them was different, including the way they viewed life.

She stopped and gazed toward the horizon, where Sean didn't have time to look—he was too busy racing toward it. She knew now why he loved his job so much, loved the confusion and excitement of bombs dropping around him, helicopters taking off and landing, bullets flying. It kept him on the move. It was his life.

But not hers. She craved security and at least a sliver of order. The scene in the kitchen the night before had been the perfect commentary on their differences. She wanted a recipe for life, while Sean thrived on a chaotic variety of ingredients.

God, they were so different. And it seemed that compromising made both of them unhappy. *That* was something they could agree on, she thought as she splashed through the tidal pools—no compromise.

So far, their first complete morning of togetherness was a disaster. She gave a moan of displeasure as she totaled imaginary scores in her head. Being in sync—failure. Sharing—failure. Talking about their differences in an attempt to solve them—failure, failure, failure.

There had to be answers, but she didn't know where to find them. In fact, she didn't even know where to begin looking.

She was sure she loved him and he loved her, or so she thought. Maybe that was the other thing they shared. Maybe neither of them knew what love was all about.

SEAN FOUND HER sitting on a sand dune, gazing at the water. He joined her and slipped his arm around her waist. "Sorry, babe."

"Me, too. I guess we're just not cut out for the morning thing."

"Don't jump to that conclusion after only one try. There'll be other mornings."

Andi chose not to respond, since he didn't sound very convincing.

"So what have you been doing?" he asked.

"Sitting. Thinking. Watching the birds."

"Ah, my bird-watching wife."

"It's interesting," she defended.

"I'm sure it is. Identify some of them for me?"

"Are you serious?"

"Of course." He kept his arm around her.

"All right. See those dark brown ones skimming over the water? Look—" she pointed "—there, the ones with white patches on their wings. They're called storm petrels. I've always loved to watch them because they seem to be dancing on the waves."

Sean nodded as enthusiastically as he could, even though he couldn't tell any difference between the petrels and the others. "I like the sound of that, dancing on the waves."

She seemed calmer to him now, more serene. This was the perfect time to share his idea to save their marriage. But for once he'd be subtle.

Taking her hand, he said, "It's great that you know so much about birds, tide pools and all those other things," he said. "You'll be able to teach our children to love nature and the outdoors."

She looked at him quizzically. "Children?"

He played with her fingers, entwining them with his. "I went to your secret place yesterday. You said it was a place you always liked to go so you could be alone and think. So I did some thinking there, too."

"You actually stopped?"

He laughed. "Well, no. I did my thinking on the run out to the point. I thought about us, where we are, where we're going. By the time I got to the point I realized how we could cement our marriage, solve our problems. It's a perfect solution and an obvious one. I'm surprised we didn't think of it before." His voice was serious and almost triumphant. "We need to have a baby."

Andi gave a strangled gasp.

"See? It surprises you, too, but it's obvious, isn't it?"

"A baby!" she said, ignoring his comment. "Where in the world did you get an idea like that?"

"I don't know," he said proudly. "It just came to me—out of my subconscious. You know," he added, "I bet seeing your sister in Clarion had something to do with it. Or maybe it's just time."

"We've never really talked about having a baby—" She seemed dazed, but Sean attributed that to the suddenness of his idea.

"We did once. Or at least we agreed that we wanted to have kids someday, remember?"

"I know, but someday isn't today!"

He took her face in his hands. "Listen, babe, this could be just what we need to make us a real family. We'll be together, raising our kid—"

"Having a baby isn't the way to save a marriage, Sean."

He looked at her, stunned at what he saw in her eyes—not a warm, welcomed commitment, but disbelief and anger. He dropped his hands.

"This will bring us closer," he said.

"But it wouldn't be right," she told him.

"Nothing is more right, Andi. You're the only woman in the world I'd want to have my child."

"Sean, what you or I want really doesn't matter. What counts is the kind of life our baby would have. We don't have a stable home. We don't even have a home! We're fighting to save our marriage. We have a long way to go, and if we're going to get there, we'll have to make it on our own."

"But we have love. Or I thought we did. Hell, Andi, nothing in life is certain. I've seen families all over the world uprooted, their houses bombed, living in tents, but they're still families. Life goes on. People have children, and they have problems. You can't control everything."

Andi stood up, walked a little away from him in the sand and then turned. "I'm not talking about everything. I'm talking about us. We can't manage to get through preparing a meal together or paddling a canoe or taking a walk with any kind of harmony. How can we rear a child?"

He waved his arms in frustration. "We just can, that's all. We will. A child is a part of life, and life is to be lived—to the fullest."

"Obviously, we have different ideas about what that means. I'm not going to have a child because of one of your whims. This is too serious, something we need to think long and hard about."

He was on his feet, too, facing her. "I had no idea when we got married that you were so rigid and stubborn," he accused. "You used to be spontaneous."

"Yeah," she shot back, "I was willing to go out to dinner at the last minute. That can hardly be compared with starting a family!"

Sean turned away in frustration. "I thought you'd jump at my idea. I can't believe your reaction."

"I can't believe your suggestion," she challenged.

"I guess you never know about a person until you live together on a deserted island."

"That's one thing we can agree on!" Her cheeks were bright, her eyes blazing. "To think that when we first met I mistook your carelessness and selfishness for charisma—"

"And I mistook your stubbornness for charm—"

"Live and learn," she said, walking away.

"Where are you going?" he shouted after her.

"Somewhere. Nowhere. For a walk."

Sean cursed loudly. "*Now* she goes for a walk." He picked up a handful of pebbles and tossed them into the bay.

SEAN WAS FURIOUS. On top of everything else, the damned radio was broken! He sat at the table and unscrewed the front plate, slowly, methodically, in an attempt to control his anger and frustration. He had no idea what he was doing. He only knew the radio had stopped working, and it was their only connection to the mainland. If he couldn't fix it, they were in deep trouble.

As he opened the radio, he carefully placed each screw, one at a time, in a pattern that duplicated the radio's innards, which he knew absolutely nothing about. He could only hope that he'd find something obvious, like a loose wire. At least if he kept the pieces in order, he'd be able to get the damned thing back together.

The broken radio was only one more sign to him that their sojourn on Pawlie's Island was doomed. Nothing good would ever happen to him in this place, he was convinced.

Andi walked into the cabin, her stubborn look still in place.

"We need to talk," she said, paying no attention to the disemboweled radio as she sank onto the sofa. "We have to decide what we're going to do."

"About lunch?" he asked, attempting a lightness he didn't feel.

"I'm serious, Sean."

"About what, then?" he asked.

"Staying here—or leaving."

Even though he'd thought the same thing himself, her words sounded ominous. Did leaving mean giving up on their marriage? He certainly didn't want that. "What do *you* want?" he asked.

"If we leave, we're saying the test is over and both of us failed. We're saying we can't make it together, and I can't bear to admit that—not yet."

"And I'll never admit it, Andi. We've only been here two days. We're having trouble adjusting, but we could work things out in another place. Even Clarion would be better than this damned island."

She looked at him sharply. "I don't agree—"

"Again," he said.

"Yes, again. I don't think another place would help us at all. Being isolated brings everything sharply into focus, illuminates all our differences—"

"Instead of looking at our differences, we ought to be searching for similarities. There're so many positives with us," Sean insisted.

"Like what?" she challenged.

His mind went blank. Then it hit him. "Sex in that big chair was pretty great." His smile was met by her frown.

"That's the point, Sean. Sex is always great."

"Well, how many people can say that? Maybe for the rest of our time here, we need to do more of it and less of the rest—"

"You want to keep trying to save the marriage?"

"Of course I do, Andi. I'd rather move to another location—" he took a deep breath "—but, yes, I want to keep on, and if this is where we have to do it, I agree. What about you?"

"I'm willing to stick out the two weeks as we planned."

"No matter what happens during that time, we stay the full two weeks?"

"Agreed. I don't give up easily, Sean."

He grinned, relieved.

Andi smiled tentatively, and for the first time seemed to notice what he was doing. "What's the problem? Dead batteries?"

"Nope. I changed the batteries yesterday and it worked. Now suddenly it doesn't. Maybe it's something in the receiving system, but I'm not sure." He suddenly realized that he'd better be sure—in order to convince Andi. "I'll just have a look."

She got up and walked to the table, glancing at the orderly line of screws. "I'm surprised you're so neat and organized. I would have expected you to jump right in. Isn't that how you repaired the television?"

"Mmm," he said noncommittally, wishing she would go away for a while. Almost as if she'd heard his wish, Andi wandered into the kitchen. Furiously, he examined the parts he'd removed one by one, finding nothing that looked as if it was out of place. "Damn," he mumbled.

"Is that you cursing again?" she asked as she came into the room, nibbling on a cookie. "Want one?" She offered him the box.

"No, thanks. And I was cussing because of this damned—pardon me—radio."

She stood by his shoulder as Sean loosened another screw, feeling all thumbs. "I'd think a TV would be much more complicated to repair than this, and you fixed it easily, didn't you?"

He answered without actually answering. "It depends on the problem." He looked inside the radio at the tubes and wiring and tried to make sense of what he was seeing, but it was hopeless—he didn't have a clue. "Tools are important, too," he added as an excuse.

"All you used in Clarion was a screwdriver." Andi sat at the table beside him. "I must admit I wondered how you got the TV fixed so easily."

"Just one of those lucky breaks." He fumbled with a screw, dropped it and reached under the table, but Andi got to it first.

"I guess it makes you nervous for me to watch," she observed, holding up the screw. "Where does this go?"

"On that pile. No, this one." He couldn't remember where the little devil had come from. "Just give it to me."

Andi complied and then went to the door and gazed at the sea. "I guess you're right about needing the shortwave radio—and not just for lobster," she added. "You never know when an emergency will happen. Like when you fell off the roof. You could have broken a leg or your neck—"

"Andi, please don't be morbid." Sean was beginning to sweat a little over the radio, which clearly had him stumped.

"Well, we need the radio, whatever happens." She looked at him with her clear brown eyes. "You can fix it, can't you?"

"Of course." Sean picked up the radio and shook it gently, alarmed at the rattling that came from inside. What the hell could that be, and how could he get to it? All he could hope for was some kind of miracle.

Andi continued to watch as he worked, no longer bothering with orderliness. Finally, he looked up and met Andi's suspicious gaze.

"Sean—"

He shrugged. "I might as well tell you that I can't fix the damn—the radio. I have no idea what's the matter with it, and there's no use pretending that I do."

"But you fixed the TV—"

"Andi, please stop it with that TV thing. I didn't fix it. I called a repairman."

Her eyes widened and darkened. "A repairman? And you pretended you did it? You deliberately lied to me, Sean, about something so . . . stupid."

"I didn't really lie, I just didn't argue when you assumed I'd done the repair—"

"Which was pretty easy to assume, since you were standing there with the screwdriver in your hand."

"It was a joke, Andi. Or a surprise. That's it. A surprise for my wife."

"And when were you planning to tell me—or were you?"

"I was waiting for the right time. Finally, when I did confess, the old Andi, the fun-loving woman I married, would have bought into the whole thing and laughed her head off."

"I don't think so. You know why?" She stood up and for a moment towered above him. "Because it isn't funny."

He stood, too, and she lost her advantage. "I think it's pretty amusing—"

"Which reinforces everything we've learned on this trip. We have nothing in common!"

"Well, I certainly can't find anything interesting about staring at puddles in the sand for hours on end. If that's your idea of fun, when you were in Rome or Barcelona or Zurich you should have had great fun, looking in all those fountains. But now you tell me you were bored all the time."

"The point is that I didn't choose to go to Rome and look at fountains. I explore the tide pools because I want to, not because you want me to." Andi realized that she'd raised her voice a few decibels, but she didn't care. "I was in Rome and all those other places because you decided that's where I should be."

"Just like you decided I'd be on this godforsaken island."

"I came here hoping to save this marriage. If it's savable," she added. "I didn't get into this marriage so I could see the great cities of Europe."

"Then why the hell did you get into it, Andi? So you and I can argue all the time?"

She felt like bursting into tears. "At this point, I really don't know, Sean. I don't know anything—except that we have a big problem. It's time for us to face reality and—"

"Wait a minute." He raised a hand to silence her. "Listen. That sounds like a motorboat."

They rushed to the porch in time to see Ed Ennis unloading something onto the pier.

"It's a lobster trap!" Andi cried. "And he's unloading something else. Oh, I hope it's food."

"Just so there's lobster," Sean said, shielding his eyes

against the sun. "Hold everything. Someone else has gotten out of the boat, and Ed's pushing off."

"Who is it?"

"A woman—"

"It's Pam, and she's coming toward the house!"

7

ANDI RAN toward the dock, slipping a little on the pine needles that covered the path.

Sean stayed back, wondering what this was all about. Right in the middle of their most heated argument, an ally arrived for Andi. One thing was sure. Pam had no great love for him, even though when they parted at the store, she'd been amiable, almost pleasant. Still, she was Andi's sister.

He started down the path, aware that Pam had sent the boat away. She'd come without being invited, and she evidently planned to stay awhile. Well, why not? Maybe she'd serve as a buffer between him and Andi.

When he got to the dock, the two women were in animated conversation, but Andi seemed as confused as he was over the unexpected visit.

"What's this all about?" she asked her sister.

"I decided you needed a lobster dinner so I caught a ride with Ed. I brought fresh corn, too. We can have an old-fashioned Maine cookout."

Andi's face still wore a puzzled look. "All this way just to deliver lobsters?"

"And to have a chat with my sister," Pam replied, maneuvering carefully to give Andi a sideways hug.

"Is something the matter?" Andi's voice showed concern. "The baby?"

Pam patted her stomach. "Kicking up a storm," she replied.

"Then what? Kevin?"

"Busy."

"And you?" Andi probed.

"I'm in great shape."

"Maybe so, but it's a very different shape. Things have definitely shifted. Are you sure the due date's still two weeks away?"

"So the doctor says." She glanced over Andi's shoulder. "Hello, Sean. Surprise—I've brought lobster."

He leaned over and dropped a quick kiss on Pam's cheek. "Best news I've heard in days."

"And fresh corn—"

"It's getting better."

"Ice—"

"The magic word," he declared.

"I remember vacations on Pawlie's, what it was like without ice. I also brought milk and cereal and eggs and bread—for me!" She grinned at her sister. "My appetite is still out of control."

"So is mine—now that I see all this food," Sean said. "I'll bring it to the house. You two go ahead."

Andi slipped her arm around Pam's shoulders. She was still surprised by her sister's sudden appearance on the island. "Who's at the store?" she asked.

"Chrissy's closing up this afternoon," Pam said, mentioning the college student who helped out in the summer months. "Tomorrow's Sunday—a holiday for everyone. On Monday, I'll radio Ed and have him pick me up."

"Maybe not," Andi muttered. "There's been a little problem with the radio."

Pam shrugged. "Kevin'll find a way to get me home." They reached the cabin, and Pam looked around with a happy smile. "It's good to be back here. The place is so quiet and restful. I'm sure you appreciate that." She climbed the stairs carefully, holding on to the rail. "Remember how you and Dad would sit at the tide pools for hours without uttering a word? I'd be running around jabbering, and you guys would be in another world."

"Times have changed," Andi said, as she remembered trying to share a quiet time with Sean.

"For me, too," Pam said. "I'm finally beginning to appreciate peace and quiet—right in time to welcome a squalling baby!"

Andi smiled as she sank onto the top step. "I showed Sean the tide pools, but it's not his thing, I guess."

"Well, it wasn't mine, either." Pam flopped onto one of the porch chairs and looked at Andi curiously. "So how's it going otherwise—with the test? Are you maybe a little discouraged?"

Andi decided to keep her troubles with Sean to herself. She was still angry over his lies about the television repair, but they certainly didn't need Pam as a referee. They'd have to finish their argument eventually, and maybe this cool-down time would be helpful.

Carefully, she answered Pam. "We've run into a few problems, but that's only natural. I mean we've never been together like this, and, well—" She struggled for the right words.

"That bad, eh?"

"We're going to keep working on things. Now," she added briskly, "let's change the subject. What's so important that you came all the way out to Pawlie's to talk?"

"Later, after we've eaten. Oh, here's Sean with the supplies. It's nice to have a man around."

"I'm glad someone thinks so," he muttered.

Andi gave a warning frown, and Sean forced a smile. Too late—Pam had seen the look. There'd be questions later about that, Andi imagined.

"I'm glad to be of help." He raised his eyebrows and glanced at Andi. "For a change."

Andi groaned. Here she was, trying to keep the problems to herself, and Sean seemed determined to tell all. Well, she wouldn't give him the opportunity. "Let's get dinner started."

"Who wants to be in charge of cooking?" Pam asked.

"I pass," Sean replied.

"I guess it's my turn," Andi volunteered.

"I'll be sure and stay out of the way," Sean said quickly.

"Good idea." Andi didn't mean to jump on him like that, but she couldn't resist.

"This is more fun than a tennis match," Pam commented. "I guess you two have had problems in the kitchen."

"Let's just say we have differing ideas about cooking," Andi replied.

"And ingredients," Sean added.

"And recipes," she countered.

"Or lack of them."

Pam laughed. "The ball's in your court, Andi."

"I forfeit," she said, forcing a smile.

"This just shows you two have become a real married couple. Kevin and I share a kitchen for about ten minutes before the fireworks. He never peels tomatoes. Can you believe that? His mother didn't, so he doesn't. I love a bacon, lettuce and tomato sandwich—but only if the tomatoes are peeled. And he's so conservative about seasoning. Imagine curried shrimp with a *touch* of curry, or chili and beans with a *teaspoon* of chili or—"

"We get the picture, Pam," Andi said.

"Well, since Kevin's not here and you two seem to need a break, why don't I cook?"

"Do you feel up to it? Maybe you should rest."

"I'm pregnant, not sick, Andi," Pam replied. "Does the grill work? I'll grill the corn, steam the lobsters and slice the French bread. How hard can that be? I even brought butter." She got up and went into the house, Sean and Andi trailing behind with the supplies.

"And don't worry about me, the doctor says I'm in great shape." Pam stopped at the living room table where the radio was still in pieces. "I see what you mean about the shortwave. Who did that?"

"I did," Sean confessed. "My attempt at repair."

Pam grinned impishly. "Looks like we need Mike Rossi here to lend a hand."

Andi gave her sister a look that could kill. But it couldn't compare with the one Sean gave her.

"I'm joking, guys," she said quickly, her brown eyes laughing.

After a long pause, Sean grinned, but Andi wasn't as generous. She marched into the kitchen, carrying her load of groceries, wondering why she'd ever suggested a Pawlie's Island marriage test—then remembering that it had been Pam's idea.

"WHAT CAN I do to help?" Sean stood in the kitchen door and watched Pam slice bread, his mouth watering. This was what he called real food—steamed lobster, grilled corn and French bread. Nothing preserved or canned, pressed, packed in oil, spiced or pickled. It was a down-home meal, but down-home with style, just what he liked.

"You can start the grill," Pam said.

"I'm a step ahead for a change. The coals are glowing," he answered.

"Want to grill the corn in the shucks?"

"Absolutely," Sean replied.

"Until they begin to turn black?"

"Right on."

"And the lobster?"

"With drawn butter," Sean suggested.

"You've got it."

Sean laughed. "See, togetherness in the kitchen can work."

"Only if you're not married to the cook. Which reminds me, where's Andi?"

"Down at the water reading a book. Or to put it another way, ignoring me."

"And me," Pam added. She buttered the loaf of bread and then looked at Sean. "So. Are you going to let me in on how this reunion is going, or have you two taken a vow of silence?"

"I've been instructed to keep everything to myself," Sean answered. "But don't tell me you haven't picked up on the overall tone."

"You're both a little touchy. That doesn't mean anything. Flare-ups in the kitchen are nothing. Then I arrived out of the blue, which was a mistake, I'm now beginning to think."

"I would have agreed with you, at first. When that boat pulled away from the dock, I was tempted to call Ed back and personally load you on it, lobster and all."

"What changed your mind?"

"I realized we needed a break. You came at just the right time. We'll get back on the right track, and eternal optimist that I am, I'm sure everything's going to work out."

Was he sure? No, but he couldn't tell Pam how afraid he was that he and Andi were on the brink of disaster. The divorce papers in Clarion still hovered over his head. And he couldn't stop hearing the words of their last argument. Why had they gotten married? Neither of them had been able to answer that. And now that they seemed to have lost so much, would they ever be able to find the magic again?

"How does Andi feel about it?"

"I have no idea. She doesn't say, and I'm not asking at this point. I used to think I knew your sister, but I'm finding out that maybe I don't."

"At least you're finding out. Which means coming here was a good move, giving you time to learn about each other."

"Yeah, but what if we don't like what we learn, Pam?"

Pam put the bread in the oven, where the fire Sean had built was going strong. "That's important, too. If it's not meant to be..."

"But it *is* meant to be," Sean insisted. "And no so-called marriage test is going to change my mind." He caught himself. "Sorry. I don't mean to drag you into this. But you're here, so you're elected."

"I don't mind. There's just one thing I'd like to ask."

"Sure."

"Could I have some of those crackers on the table? I'm starving, and I can't wait for dinner."

Sean laughed as he opened a package and handed her a cracker.

"More," she said.

"Let me make it a real treat." He opened a jar of caviar and began spreading it on crackers.

"What's that smell?"

"Caviar. Beluga—the best." He handed her a plate full of crackers piled high with caviar. "Wait'll you taste this."

"Ugh. Get it away!"

"Pam, this is the world's top caviar. You have to taste it."

She leaned against the counter, hands to her mouth. "If you don't get it away, I'm going to faint."

"No, don't!" Sean said.

"Or throw up."

Sean tossed the plate into the trash, but she was already beginning to sway. He reached for her and she sagged against him.

"Andi," he yelled. "Get up here—now!"

ANDI HEARD THE CALL even above the splashing waves. She dropped her book and raced to the cabin. When she burst into the living room, Pam was on the sofa, and Sean was kneeling beside her.

"What'll we do?" Sean asked helplessly. Pam was ghostly pale. But at least she hadn't fainted—not quite, anyway—or thrown up.

"I'll get a wet cloth."

Pam was half-sitting when she came back with the cloth, which she laid against her sister's forehead.

"I'm okay," Pam said, but her response was feeble.

"Lean forward," Andi advised. As Pam obeyed, putting her head between her knees, Andi questioned Sean across her limp form. "What happened?"

"She turned white and said she felt like she was going to faint or—"

"I'm not going to do either now," Pam told them, cocking her head.

Andi pushed it gently between her knees. "Keep down until the dizziness passes."

"It's passed," Pam insisted, sitting up. "I'm perfectly all right."

"Something's wrong or you wouldn't have nearly fainted."

Pam leaned back in the chair. "I was woozy from the trip, and I was hungry."

"But when I tried to get you to eat—"

"Sean, if you'd ever been pregnant you'd know that some things are very unappealing in the food department. Number one for me is caviar, which I'm not all that fond of under the best of circumstances."

"I hope that's all it was," Andi said.

"I guarantee I'll be fine as soon as I have some food—of the non-fish-egg variety."

"I'll finish dinner. You stay put," Andi ordered, heading into the kitchen.

"Put the top on that caviar jar," Pam called after her.

"NOW THAT WAS a meal," Sean complimented as he pushed back from the table an hour later. "I can honestly say the best we've had on the island."

"I second that." Andi looked at her sister. "You certainly gobbled down everything on your plate. But you still look a little pale to me."

"It's left over from the caviar experience."

"It's a good lesson for Sean. Not everyone in the world is crazy for fish eggs."

"Maybe not, but to tell the truth, I still can't believe I threw away that entire plate of caviar," he said.

"You threw it away?" Andi asked.

"I didn't stop to think about alternatives. Pam looked very weird, and she definitely didn't want it anywhere near."

"Let's change the subject, if you don't mind," Pam pleaded.

"Okay, let's have that talk you promised, Pam," Andi said. "If you're up to it."

"I'm up to anything, but I'm not sure now's the time to . . ."

"Sounds like girl talk," Sean said, standing up. "I'll take care of the dishes. You two do the sister thing."

"No, Sean," Pam said. "You probably should hear this, because it concerns you, too, indirectly."

"Uh-oh." Andi sank back in her chair. "What is it?"

"I think you just guessed. It's the store. I called the real estate broker yesterday and told her to take it off the market."

"Pam, you didn't! We already have prospects lined up."

"Doesn't matter. We can't sell unless we both agree." She sat up as straight as she could, considering her condition, and said emphatically, "I don't agree."

"We've been through this a million times. The store needs two full-time people. One person, especially a pregnant person—"

"I won't be pregnant forever."

"Especially a person with a baby," Andi corrected herself. "One person can't do it all. Stocking and buying is a full-time job. Then there's staffing, book-keeping—"

"I've worked in the store since I was twelve, as you well know," Pam interrupted.

"When you were twelve, you weren't running the place. Besides, there were three other people—your parents and your sister. Mom and Dad are gone, I'm leaving, and you're having a baby. Get real, Pam. It can't be done."

"If I can interrupt," Sean said. "I know it's none of my business, but why can't Pam hire a manager? It's done all the time in retail."

Andi was ready for that. "We've tried. Kent Unlimited is a seasonal company with many down months. It doesn't pay to hire someone who'd sit around half the time. It's just not satisfactory."

"Well, satisfactory or not, it'll have to do until the baby is old enough—" Pam began.

"Which brings us to the other problem," Andi went on, "finding—and keeping—a reliable sitter."

"I won't need a sitter." Pam looked smug. "The baby will go to the store with me."

"It won't work," Andi said emphatically. "You can't rear a baby and run a store, especially if you have to depend on erratic part-time help. And *I'm* certainly not going to stick around Clarion." She shot a look at Sean. "Whatever happens."

Pam's round face reddened. "I don't get your attitude, Andi. The store is a part of our family, and nothing in the world is more important than family. I could no more sell Kent Unlimited than I could sell Pawlie's Island."

"Then why did you agree to it before?" Andi asked.

"Your argument was so strong and you were so sure of yourself that I went along with you. Now I've had time to think, and if you're honest with yourself, you'll agree with me. Our store is a legacy for our children and their children." She paused and glanced over, a little superior, Andi thought. "When you have kids of your own, you'll feel the same way."

Andi avoided Sean's long, cool stare. "I can understand your feelings without benefit of my own baby, Pam. But we have to be practical—"

"Maybe I could buy you out," Pam offered, a little weakly.

Andi didn't bother to respond. Pam and Kevin couldn't afford that solution, and they both knew it.

"Pam, we've talked and talked about this. And we both agreed that the best—the only—solution is to sell the store so I can get on with my life and you can concentrate on your family. We don't need to discuss it."

"Yes, we do, because I've changed my mind!" Pam cried.

"Great, and now everything is upside down again, which is becoming the norm for my screwed-up life."

Sean made a point of getting up then to clear the table. The two women watched him silently, and when he spoke his voice was casual. "Life can't be controlled all that easily, Andi, as I told you before. Human beings have a way of screwing things up."

Pam looked at him, her eyes wide. "Does that mean you agree with me?"

"That means it's your life, honey. You have to make your own choices. If you want the store, then go for it."

Andi threw up her hands. "And ignore the consequences? Am I the only person who thinks ahead around here?"

She was met by two noncommittal gazes.

"I'm going to bed," Andi said suddenly.

"It's only nine o'clock," Pam objected.

"What of it? I refuse to sit here and argue just because it's not time for bed. I'm not sleepy, but I feel a killer headache coming on, which is making me extremely irritable. I'm going upstairs because if I stay here one more minute I'll say something I regret."

She turned and stormed up the stairs.

Sean looked at Pam with a frown. "A new side of your sister is revealed."

Pam pulled herself up from the table. "Not for me. I'm used to these little battles. As kids we argued all the time. Doors slammed in our house on a regular basis. Believe me, she'd have slammed a door just now, except there isn't one!"

Sean couldn't resist a smile.

"She'll be fine tomorrow, but at least I made my point."

"You sure did," Sean agreed.

The two allies, an odd couple, to be sure, Sean decided, cleared the table, and when Pam suggested a game of gin rummy, Sean agreed quickly. He'd never been to sleep at this time of night, and wasn't going to start now.

WHEN HE CLIMBED into bed beside Andi, she stirred and groaned irritably.

"Sorry to wake you," he said.

"I was already awake," she answered.

"How're you feeling?"

"My head's still pounding."

"Better take a couple of aspirin."

"What a concept," she replied sarcastically. "I took three already." She scrunched up, pulling her legs to her chest.

Sean had never seen her in this mood. In an odd way, it excited him, seeing her sleepy, irritable, her cheeks flushed and her hair tangled around her face. The moonlight that seemed to have followed them throughout their trip spilled across her face. She looked exotic—and very beautiful.

"I can think of one thing that would help."

"What?" she asked with another moan.

He put his lips next to her ear and whispered, "Love, love, love."

She rolled over and looked at him. "Are you serious?"

"'Course. We've made love in lots of places on the island, but never in the obvious place—our bed."

She leaned on one elbow. The moonlight was bright enough for her to make out his strong, handsome features. "You and I are in the midst of a very important discussion—"

"Argument," he corrected her.

"Whatever. Until we resolve our differences, there's no place for romance."

"Then let's resolve one issue right now. I'm sorry I made up the story about the TV repair, but it's not a felony, Andi. I won't go to jail for it. Actually, it's kind of amusing—"

Andi turned her back on him and pounded her pillow. "There's nothing funny about it."

"I'm sorry. That was the wrong thing to say."

She looked at him over her shoulder. "It doesn't matter, Sean, because it's not the lie that hurts. It's not even the fact that I feel like a fool for falling for it. The lie is just the tip of the iceberg. It's the principle of the thing."

"Why do women always say that?" he asked. "The principle of the thing."

"Why do men never know what we're talking about?"

"Because you're more complex than we are?" he offered with a smile.

She managed not to smile back. "Probably. Principles mean a lot. But to get down to simple terms that you can understand, Sean—the test is a failure, the trip is a failure, and to top it all, Pam has blindsided me about the store."

"It means a lot to her. Maybe it's not such a bad idea."

"Are you and Pam ganging up on me?"

"Of course not, Andi. I guess what I'm saying is that she's not your baby sister anymore. She's a grown woman about to have a child of her own. In a lot of ways she's more mature than we are."

"Speak for yourself," Andi replied.

Sean stretched and yawned. "All right. Speaking for myself, I'm still aching for you." He nuzzled her hungrily. "Throbbing for you." He pulled her close. "I'm still—"

"Stop," she cautioned before he got more graphic. "Keep your voice down. Pam can hear you through the walls. They're like paper."

"So that's it. You don't want her to hear our strangled cries of passion as I please you—" he rolled over and snuggled against her back, spoonlike "—with my lips." He kissed the back of her neck. "And my hands." He slid his arm around her and touched her breast.

She squirmed away. "Stop it."

"Why?"

She wiggled toward her side of the bed. "I told you, romance is the last thing on my mind."

"Okay, okay, but how about a compromise?"

"That always gets us in trouble."

"I'll just hold you." He cautiously put his arm around her waist. "You need to be held, Andi. I know I do."

He felt her relax against him as she gave out a long sigh. "I'd like that," she said.

He lifted her slightly and slipped his other arm under her.

"Let's declare a truce," she offered. "At least until Pam leaves. Then we can think about us and our future."

He pulled her closer, cradling her in his arms and settling her against the curve of his body. "Truce it is."

SUNDAY MORNING dawned bright and fair. The wind kicked up in the bay and tousled Andi's hair riotously about her head as she walked to the water with her shovel and pail.

"Going to build some sand castles?" Sean asked as he caught up with her.

She attempted a withering look. "No, I thought I'd just play in the sand for a while," she said sarcastically. She put down the bucket, planted her shovel in the sand and turned toward him. "I'm digging for clams for chowder tonight."

"Need some help?" he offered.

"No, thanks. You go ahead and run. I know how important your morning exercise is to you."

"It doesn't seem all that important this morning," he said.

She shrugged, grabbed the shovel and started to dig.

Sean watched her for a little while before giving up and starting his run—away from the beach, toward the meadow where he'd wanted to run the day before. Today he could run where he chose, without advice from Andi. Still, he started out with a heavy heart.

Andi concentrated on her digging and didn't hear her sister approach across the sand. "Need some help?" She put down her camp chair and sank heavily into it with a deep sigh.

Andi turned and looked at her, laughing.

"All right. I'm not going to dig, but I can cheer you on. If we want enough clams for chowder, someone's going to have to give you a hand. Where's Sean?"

"On his run."

"So you're skipping morning time on your famous test?"

"Mmm," Andi said, noncommittally.

"That's probably a smart thing to do—stay away from each other in the a.m."

Andi stopped digging, tossed a clam into her bucket and looked at her sister. "We tried the morning thing, and it was a bad experience. Maybe by the end of this—this . . ." She struggled for the words.

"Vacation?" Pam prompted.

"No, I wouldn't call it that."

"Honeymoon?"

Andi laughed. "Definitely not that. Ordeal is more like it, or at least trial by error. Anyway, maybe by the end of this we'll be in sync." She started digging again. "Probably not."

"Somehow, I didn't think he'd pass your test."

Andi noticed there was no malice in Pam's words, only a calm acceptance.

"Maybe the guy just isn't cut out for the role. Some of them aren't. They make great lovers but awful husbands. Too bad, because I kinda like him, since he's on my side about the store." She added thoughtfully, "I like him anyway. But he's definitely not husband material."

Andi went on digging, not anxious to continue a discussion with Pam about her marriage. On the other hand, she didn't want to argue about the store, either. She felt hemmed in and pressured from all sides. Only from above did she sense a kind of peace. She looked at the puffy clouds in the dark blue sky. The cry of a storm petrel sounded on the breeze. It was soothing, somehow. She watched the bird swoop and dance over the waves, her eyes following longingly.

"Wouldn't it be wonderful," she said, half to herself, "to be that free? To forget everything and fly away into the unknown? To be free of cares and of—"

"Sean?" Pam finished. "And your baby sister? What did you call me—grouchy?"

"I'd forgotten what sharp ears you have." Andi dug up a couple of clams and tossed them into the bucket.

"Yep, I could always hear what you and your boyfriend were whispering on the back porch."

"Because you spied, let's face it," Andi said.

"Why not, when you'd end up bribing me not to tell Mom and Dad."

Andi put down the shovel and sat in the sand by her sister. "And you never did tell."

"Nope. I was a good sister. Still am, even though I don't agree with you about the store." Pam touched her shoulder. "I know you're angry with me."

"No, I'm not angry, but I'm certainly not happy. I think it's a bad idea, but I can't do anything about it because you have me boxed in. We can't sell unless we both agree."

Pam tilted her face toward the warmth of the sun. "Don't try to change things, Andi. Just go with the flow. You don't need the money at this point."

"No, I don't," Andi agreed.

"So wait it out with us. If I can't make it, we sell, and you haven't lost anything. Meanwhile, you'll share the profits. Either I can do it or not. Time will tell."

Andi sighed and leaned back on her elbows. "So how'd you get so philosophical all of a sudden?"

"Maybe it's impending motherhood."

"Doesn't it scare you to death? The motherhood thing?"

"Mmm, sometimes. Especially at first, but now I'm excited. It's going to be a wonderful adventure, rearing a child."

"Sean was right," Andi commented. "You are more grown-up than I am—at least about this. The thought of taking care of a baby scares me to death. Sean and I aren't ready. I wonder if we ever will be."

"You and Sean are different from Kevin and me. You've had a very romantic, adventurous marriage, jet-setting around the world—"

"Where I usually ended up sitting alone in some elegant but miserable hotel."

"Some people would think that was exciting."

"So did I. For the first few months."

"Well, it's hard for me to imagine, since it's so different from the life Kevin and I have led since we first met—"

"In kindergarten," her sister reminded her.

"Remember when I decided to marry him?"

Andi stopped to think. "Ninth grade?"

"Eighth. Let's say we've had long enough to get used to each other's habits, bad and good."

"Which we're trying to do in two weeks," Andi commented as Sean appeared in the distance.

He ran at the water's edge, and both women watched in fascination. The muscles of his legs contracted and expanded as he ran, and his arms moved gracefully in perfect rhythm. He splashed in the water and then veered away, creating a perfect ribbon of movement.

Andi shaded her eyes and looked up as he approached them. He was bare-chested, his golden-hued skin gleaming damply in the sunlight, the light dusting of hair along his chest silken and shimmering. Breathing hard, he shook his tawny hair and smiled at them.

Dammit, he was beautiful, Andi thought, her breath catching in her throat—tall and golden, like a young god. Each time she saw him it was like the first time all over again. Maybe what Pam said made sense—they were meant to be lovers but never man and wife.

"Good morning," he said, dropping onto the sand beside Pam. "We're roughing it, so I didn't shave." He rubbed the golden stubble on his chin. "Hope you don't mind."

"Not a bit," Pam said. "Pawlie's is a place to take life easy." She stretched lazily, digging her heels into the sand.

"Where'd you run?" Andi asked.

"I found a way to get to the meadow through the pines. Then up to your secret place. Where I did some more deep thinking," he added, smiling at her.

Pam eyed them quizzically. Andi wasn't going to be happy about that, Sean decided, and quickly commented, "The wind's building up. It'll be a great day for sailing."

"It already is," Andi observed. "Look at all the boats in the bay."

In the distance, sailboats skimmed the waves, their white sails filling as they caught the wind.

"Do you think there's a race going on? Those three to the south are definitely in competition," Pam said.

"But look, that big one is heading toward Pawlie's," Andi commented.

They watched as one of the boats tacked, caught the wind and sped toward Pawlie's Island. Its sails billowed against the sky like a great seabird.

Sean stood up and gave Pam a hand. She struggled to a standing position. Andi dropped her shovel and stood beside them. They watched silently as the big sailing boat came closer and closer.

"It's going to dock!" Pam exclaimed. "Let's check it out."

The threesome headed for the dock.

"That boat looks familiar," Andi commented. "Very familiar." She looked wide-eyed at her sister. "Do you think—"

"I do," Pam answered as they hurried toward the dock. "It's Mike's boat."

"What the hell is *he* doing here?" Sean asked.

"I have no idea," Andi replied, "any more than I know why *your* mother is standing on the deck of *his* boat."

8

THEY STOOD on the dock and watched the sailboat approach with Mike at the tiller. He brought the boat alongside and tossed a rope to Andi.

On the bow, tall and elegant, leaning forward a little, like an ancient ship's carved figurehead, was Reena Fleming. As the boat docked, she turned toward the shore, smiled slightly and lifted a braceleted arm in greeting to a stunned Sean, puzzled Pam and noncommittal Andi, who had grabbed the line and was busy tying off the boat.

Sean stepped forward as his mother debarked.

"Mother?"

Reena didn't seem to notice his surprise as she balanced with one foot on the boat, the other on the dock. "Yes, it's your mother. Give me a hand, son. And then I'll welcome a hug from you."

Sean lifted Reena onto the dock and hugged her affectionately. "This is quite a surprise," he said. "Why are you—"

"Here?" she finished for him as she lifted her chin dramatically. Sean had seen that gesture often in recent years. It served to smooth away the wrinkles. She adjusted her designer sunglasses and smiled again, her ruby red lips shining with the latest in cosmetic gloss.

"Why, I'm here to see you, my darling—and her," she added, nodding toward Andi, "of course."

Sean noted that her nautical blue slacks and jacket fitted perfectly and were still crisp and unwrinkled. She was clearly dressed for an outing and probably didn't realize that Pawlie's Island wasn't the yacht club setting she expected.

"And I'm here thanks to Mike," she added, gesturing to her skipper, who was still on board, furling the sails.

Andi, having secured her rope, approached her mother-in-law.

"Andi, dear." Reena put her hand lightly on Andi's arm and made a kissing sound near her cheek.

"Reena," Andi replied, raising her eyebrow to Sean, who shrugged.

"And there's our mother-to-be," Reena said as she moved down the dock toward Pam.

"What's this all about?" Andi whispered.

"I have no idea," Sean answered. "Rossi's your friend."

"And Reena's *your* mother."

Mike joined them on the dock. His initial move to greet Andi affectionately was halted by a glowering frown from Sean.

"Fleming," Mike said curtly.

"Rossi," came the cool response.

Mike turned his attention to Andi. "So this is the Pawlie's Island that I've seen from the distance so many times. Glad to be here, finally."

"With Reena?" Andi's comment was put in the form of a question.

Mike flashed a smile, his teeth gleaming against his perfect tan. "She wanted to come over. I was there," he answered simply.

Mike wore white shorts and shirt, spotless even after sailing from the mainland, which made Sean uncomfortably aware of his own appearance—a half-clothed beach bum standing before the admiral of the fleet.

Andi noticed the difference in the men's looks, but she wasn't turned off by Sean's sweat-stained running shorts, shaggy hair or burgeoning beard. He looked rugged and vital. She barely noticed Mike's crisp, cool demeanor as she questioned him.

"How did you know who Reena was or what she was doing here?"

"She came looking for me," Mike said as he secured a second rope from the stern. "Didn't you, Reena?"

"They told me at Kent's where you'd gone," she said, gazing at her son. "So I decided to find someone to bring me."

Mike smiled widely. "It was a great day for sailing."

"Well, that's very...nice," Andi stammered.

Sean said nothing.

"We'll give you lunch and maybe a short tour of the island," Andi went on, thinking furiously of a way to get them on the boat before the end of the day.

"Don't worry about feeding us," Mike said. "We brought lunch—lots of it. Why don't you give me a hand, Fleming?"

Sean gritted his teeth, not prepared to give any more than a hand to this disgustingly immaculate sailor. He took the basket and heavy cooler handed to him and turned toward the house as Andi gave him a helpless smile.

She moved to join Pam and Reena, thinking that maybe this could be a good omen, after all. The same sailboat that brought Sean's mother to Pawlie's Island could take her back—and take Pam with her. Then Andi and Sean could get on with their lives, their marriage—and their test. If they still had the heart for it.

When she caught up with them, Reena had her arm around Pam, her head bent close, chatting animatedly. She turned to Andi. "We've been catching up on news." Andi looked past Reena at Pam, who shrugged helplessly. "I haven't seen you girls since your Dad's funeral, you know. We're family, and yet we're rarely together."

Andi caught the implied rebuke. "That's true," she admitted.

It *was* true that she'd made no effort to see Reena in the past six months, but there was certainly reason for that. It would have been very awkward, trying to find something to talk about. She imagined a conversation that began, "Sorry, Reena, but I'm planning to divorce your son."

She smiled wryly and veered onto another course. "Now we have a chance to get to know each other better. We have all day." Andi could be very friendly—for a day. "So let's enjoy ourselves. Come on, I'll show you the cabin."

The women walked single file up the path. "I know this visit is a big surprise," Reena said.

"Yes, we—" Andi began to say.

Reena cut off her response. "But it's a good one, I hope. It was very difficult for me, knowing Sean was in the country and not seeing him. So I thought, why not a little visit? There's nothing wrong with a mother wanting to see her son." She added quickly, "And her daughter-in-law. I knew you wouldn't mind sharing him for a while."

Andi sighed. Reena had an uncanny way of answering unasked questions and then anticipating responses to her answers. The woman was a talker, not a listener. Andi decided to go with the flow.

"Here's the cabin, Reena," she said, pretty sure that statement couldn't be doubted, since the cottage stood solidly before them.

Reena pulled off her sunglasses, and Andi was struck with how trim and attractive she was. At fifty-five, Reena looked ten years younger, blond with a stylish figure. But in spite of the sprightliness of her step, the gaiety of her smile and her constant cheerful chatter, there was an air of dissatisfaction and unrest about her. Andi had the feeling her mother-in-law was looking for something that she had long ago given up hope of finding.

"Well, isn't this quaint?" Reena trilled. "So cozy and . . ." She walked up the steps and peered inside.

"And primitive," Andi finished. "The house is meant to be rustic."

"Hmm," was Reena's comment.

"This was our family hideaway, a place far from the trappings of civilization," she explained.

Sean came up the path from the dock and joined them. "The Kents believed in tradition, Mom. This place has a lot of sentimental value to Andi and Pam."

"And, of course, it's absolutely charming," Reena declared.

"It's not the Hamptons or Cape Cod," Pam said with a laugh, holding open the door for Sean and Mike. They struggled in under the weight of coolers and hampers of food. "Which is what people expect. So they're sometimes surprised."

"Right about that," Sean mumbled.

"Well, *I'm* surprised that you and Andi would pick this kind of place for your reunion," Reena said to her son as she followed him into the living room.

"I suppose it's possible to get back to basics here," Mike said, thumping his cooler on the floor. "But it's one hell of a place for a marriage test."

Andi winced when Mike blurted out the words. She turned to look at Sean, dreading his expression, which was bright with anger.

"You know about the marriage test?" Sean asked. When he got only a silent nod, he turned his angry gaze to Reena.

"I didn't say a word to Mike," she defended herself. "He knew all about it when I ran into him in town."

Sean turned to Andi. "Thanks a lot," he said bitterly, "for spreading our personal business all over New England."

"It wasn't me," Andi defended herself quickly, looking from Sean to Mike and finally at Pam.

Mike and Reena followed her gaze. Now three pairs of eyes were centered on Pam.

"You're the only one left," Sean said.

"Okay, I confess, Sean. I mentioned it to Mike in town. I didn't realize you two were so sensitive. But I found out pretty quickly. Andi has already chewed me out once."

Sean could hardly vent his anger on his pregnant sister-in-law, so he spoke to the room in general. "The test was private—and personal—at one time," he said.

"I didn't know that, Fleming," Mike said. "But you might as well face it, the test isn't private now."

"So," Reena said pertly. "Now that it's out in the open, how's it going?"

"Fine," Sean said. "Just fine."

"Well, I think it's a silly idea, anyway. No offense, Andi. But really, testing your husband—as if love could be measured. I can't imagine."

"Neither can I," Sean replied softly.

No one seemed to hear him except Andi, and she'd had enough. "Much of the test is unimaginable," she commented, "but it's also personal, between me and Sean." She turned and headed toward the kitchen. "So why don't we just go onto other subjects, such as lunch?"

"Isn't it a little early for lunch?" Reena asked.

"Not at all. This day's been so long, I'm beginning to think it must be time for dinner," Andi murmured.

"Hey, what's this?" Mike asked, catching sight of the radio on the table. "What happened, did someone drop it off a cliff?"

"No," Sean said coolly. "I tried to fix it."

Mike picked up a couple of pieces. "Unsuccessfully," he commented.

"Very astute," Sean said.

"You don't understand, Fleming. This can't be repaired because it's too far gone. Looks to me as if it wore out from old age. See how these terminals are corroded? And the wiring is unraveling. This baby is shot, for sure. I'm surprised you thought it could be fixed."

Before Sean could answer, Andi, pausing at the kitchen door, jumped in defensively. "He had to give it a try, obviously. We were stranded here without a radio."

"Can *you* fix it, Mike?" Pam asked.

"No way. I doubt if a rocket scientist could repair this."

Sean, pulling on a clean shirt, gave a little smirk of vindication.

"I have an extra shortwave in my boat," Mike told him. "Always carry a spare. I'll leave it here for you—if you want me to," he offered.

"Yes, we do," Andi replied, "don't we, Sean?"

"If this one can't be repaired, then we do. Thanks, Rossi," he said.

Andi smiled against her will. So far two bombs had been defused—the marriage test and the radio.

"Bring out the food," Pam suggested. "I'm hungry."

"As always," Andi said almost gaily as she opened containers.

"I wonder if I'll be this into food after the baby comes. Right now I'm as big as a whale and still eating."

"Don't worry," Reena advised her confidently. "The weight will drop right off. I was back in a size eight a month after Sean was born."

Pam laughed. "I haven't been a size eight since I was ten years old, so that won't happen to me."

Reena opened a carton of potato salad and dished it into a serving bowl, which Andi had brought from the kitchen, along with plates, utensils, napkins and the rest.

"Babies are so wonderful, aren't they?" Reena asked, without, as usual, waiting for a response. "I'd love to be a grandmother. Of course, Andi and Sean would have to cooperate." She smiled brightly at her son, generously including Andi in her smile.

Sean opened a bottle of beer.

Andi laid out place settings.

Reena continued undeterred. "There's nothing like a baby to bring joy to a marriage."

Sean's philosophy exactly, Andi thought, knowing she should keep her mouth shut, but the words popped out. "*If* the marriage is a healthy one." She ripped into a package of cold cuts. "Bologna, anyone?"

Reena turned her attention to Pam. "It's so refreshing to see a young woman like you choosing to have a child. So many women are only interested in their careers."

Andi deliberately kept her head down and her mouth closed, wondering what Sean had told his mother. That she was the stereotypical career woman, no doubt. That she didn't want him or a family, definitely. Could he have run the baby idea by his mother first?

Mike sat at the table. "Don't you think women should have careers, Mrs. Fleming?"

"Well, I don't know about careers, but I suppose they should work—if they have to, and possibly if they want to." She gave a little laugh. "I didn't work, of course. I was so busy rearing Sean and being a wife that I never had a chance for a career."

Pam piled potato salad high on her plate. "I'll be doing both, taking care of the family and running the store. May I have some potato chips?"

Mike handed her the bag. "You're not selling Kent's?"

"It's a long story," Andi put in.

"But I'm interested. What's going on?" Mike persisted.

Pam looked questioningly at Andi, who shrugged. "Sure," she said. "Tell them. I'm going down to the dock to check my knots. My seamanship isn't what it used to be." She was desperately grasping for an excuse to get away. "I don't want the boat to drift," she explained to Mike.

"I can do it," he offered.

"No, go ahead with lunch, you and Reena—and Pam, of course. Maybe Sean can help me."

Sean was already at the door. As he opened it, Reena called, "As long as you're going down to the boat, will you bring my suitcase up? It's the tan travel case."

Sean stared at her. "Suitcase?"

"Well, you didn't think I'd come all this way and not spend a few days with you when there's plenty of room." She paused while Sean just stood looking at her, dumbfounded. "There's room, isn't there?"

ON THE PORCH, Sean grabbed Andi's arm. "We need to talk."

"Come down to the dock," Andi suggested.

"You actually have to tie the boat? I thought that was just an excuse to get out of there."

"It was," she admitted, "but I'm not the sailor I once was, and I'd hate for that boat to float away—and leave all these people behind."

Sean laughed. "I'm with you."

He waited on the dock while Andi climbed into the boat and checked the lines. "It's really blowing out there," she said as she looked toward the bay, where the wind had grown stronger, creating whitecaps on the surface of the blue-green sea.

"Need some help?"

"No," she said, "I've got it." She dropped onto the dock and looked at him. "Now, what was all that baby stuff from Reena?"

"I have no idea. I'm not responsible for what my mother says or does, and I've certainly never talked to her about us having kids—or not."

"Well, since she's going to stay with us, I guess you'd better get her travel case."

"No way," Sean answered. "I love my mother, and I'd like to spend a little time with her—at some point. But not here. Not now. Besides, she has no idea what we mean by primitive. Once she checks out the place, she'll change her mind about staying. Can you just see her showering in the outdoor facilities?"

"Or lighting the wood-burning stove?"

"Or reading by candlelight? She stays up half the night, you know, reading romance novels—"

"But she manages very well in daylight," Andi told him, "and right now it looks like she's coming after us."

"What?"

Andi looked at the house, where Reena was standing on the porch, shielding her eyes with her hand, looking toward the boat.

"Oh, no. There come the other two behind her. And you're right, they're heading this way," he said.

"So much for our talk."

"No, Andi. We're going to have that talk. Somewhere else."

"Where?"

"How about your secret place?"

"Think we can get there without them seeing us?"

"The sun's in our favor," he replied. "Come on."

He took her hand, ran for the end of the dock and jumped to the sand.

"Head for the cove," Andi cried.

They ran along the beach, dodging jagged rocks and jumping tide pools. Andi looked over her shoulder once, to see Reena leading the others along the path toward the dock. "They don't see us," she said, panting. "Can we slow down?"

"Not until we get to your place." Sean kept up the pace, dragging Andi along.

"I'm glad I didn't go jogging with you the other morning," she said. "You don't jog—you tear across the beach like an Olympic sprinter."

"Only when there's danger of being followed." He finally slowed, then stopped as they approached the headland. Twenty feet above the sea was the sheltered spot, surrounded by large boulders. Andi's secret place.

She led the way to a path on the other side, and they climbed easily and settled into a smooth place hollowed from the rock.

Taking time to let Andi catch her breath, Sean said, "Now about my mother's advice—"

"On having a baby?" Andi completed. She shook her head. "This isn't the right time for family therapy sessions."

Sean agreed. "And we're certainly not opening a bed and breakfast, especially for our families."

"Not with so much unsettled between us," she added.

"For once we agree," he said lightly. "But it'll be difficult for me to tell Reena to leave while Pam stays."

"No problem. Pam isn't staying."

Sean lifted his eyebrows.

"That's the beauty of it. She can sail back with Mike and Reena. We'll suggest it in a tactful and loving way—"

Sean grinned. "Like, 'Get off our island, folks, so we can continue to fight'?"

"But we're not fighting," she reminded him.

He smiled at her. "That's one good thing about having guests. It tones down our hostility level considerably."

"We're okay as long as we're surrounded by guests—or making love," Andi commented.

He put his arm around her.

"Unfortunately, the rest of the time it doesn't seem to work." Andi leaned her head against the giant boulder. "Maybe Pam was right when she said you made a great boyfriend but a terrible husband."

"I'll remember to thank her," he said dryly.

"She meant it in a complimentary way," Andi teased.

"I'm working at it, Andi. Yesterday we got along only when we were making love. Today we're getting along surrounded by guests. Little by little, we'll get along in other situations. Or not," he said wryly.

Andi laughed. "Maybe we just aren't cut out for marriage. I have to share responsibility for that, Sean. I'm not the greatest of wives."

"I disagree, but that's for later. For now, we've got my mother, your sister and the remarkable handyman Mike Rossi to take care of."

"This is turning into a French farce."

"Next we'll have relatives jumping out of closets."

Andi giggled at the thought before adding more seriously, "We have to tell them something, Sean. What?"

"The truth. That you and I need to be alone to figure out how we're going to make it." He looked at her seriously. "Or *if* we're going to make it. It's that simple."

"Isn't it also a little selfish?" she wondered.

"Maybe, but if there was ever a time for selfishness, it's now." He helped her to her feet and held her close for a moment. He'd missed her softness. It made his head spin, and it gave him ideas about what else they could be doing, what they did best. "Andi, let's just forget about what's happening down there at the cabin . . ."

Andi shook her head. "How can we forget it? Your mother, my sister and—"

"The inevitable handyman. Yeah, you're right. I guess it's not time to resume our test."

"This is going to be test enough. Us against them."

"Maybe our most important test so far," Sean said softly.

"HERE WE GO," Sean murmured as they strode into the cabin. "Facing the lions."

"Well," Reena pronounced, breathing out a stream of air with the single syllable, stretching it into two. "There you are. You weren't on the dock, at all."

"Sure we were, Mom. Andi tied down the boat."

"But you didn't get my suitcase. I brought that up myself. Andi," she added brightly. "Mike brought one of his shortwave radios for you. Since you don't have your own. We've been listening to it and—"

"Speaking of listening," Sean said, reaching for Andi's hand and squeezing it, "I'd appreciate it if you'd listen to what Andi and I have to say." He cleared his throat, but before he could go on, Pam came out of the kitchen.

"Did you hear about the storm?"

Sean breathed a deep sigh. Clearly, he'd lost their attention—if he'd ever had it.

"Yeah, there's bad weather blowing in from the northeast," Mike confirmed. "I picked up the warnings when I was testing the shortwave."

That's when Andi caught her breath. The last thing they wanted was for Mike, Reena and Pam to be stranded in the cabin with her and Sean. "It'll be safe for you to cross," she said, making the statement that should have been a question but was a prayer.

"Sure," Mike said. "The bay is really kicking up, but the storm's still hours away. I'll make it back easily—if I get going right away."

Sean and Andi looked at each other, trying to conceal their grins. The storm was a gift from heaven.

"Then I guess that breaks up our party," Sean said. "You ladies won't want to be stuck out here in a storm. You'd better sail back with Mike."

"Not me," Pam exclaimed, heading for the sofa. "I wouldn't get on that boat for anything, not the way I'm feeling."

"What are you talking about?" Andi couldn't believe her ears. "You swore that you were feeling fine."

"That was before."

"Before?"

"Lunch. I ate too much, and now I'm feeling really strange. I couldn't possibly face those big waves, Andi." Her big brown eyes met Andi's pleadingly.

"Surely you don't expect that child to go out in a storm," Reena began.

"There's no storm yet," Sean said. "There's only a *wind*."

"But it'll eventually build into a storm," Andi added. "And you'll be caught in it if you don't leave soon."

"There's nothing to be afraid of, Reena," Sean assured his mother.

"I'm not afraid, but I don't relish getting into a tiny boat—"

"It's not tiny," Mike said defensively.

Andi and Sean both gave him a smile of gratitude.

"It's *very small*," Reena said. "And the sea is very large, and the wind is blowing very hard." She turned toward Sean. "Besides, I didn't come here to turn around and go back. I've come here to spend time with my son . . . and his wife, of course. Now you're trying to toss me out the door—and a pregnant girl with me. Well, I must say—"

"Mother, don't be so dramatic. Andi and I just want a little time to ourselves."

"We've only been here for three days. We came to spend time together," Andi said.

"Alone," Sean added. "While we work out our problems."

"Oh, yes. The marriage test," Reena said with a disdainful sniff.

"No, Reena. This is about us," Sean said firmly. "We need to work on *us*. And we need to do it alone," he muttered.

Pam, from her position on the sofa, called out, "How can one more night make any difference? The storm will be over tomorrow, and then Ed will come for me. He can take Reena back, too."

"His lobster boat is much smaller than Mike's sailboat," Andi muttered.

"But the sea will be calm tomorrow," Reena said. "A storm's coming today, and I want dry land under my feet."

Pam laughed. "Me, too. But they're trying to send us out on a wet ocean."

Andi and Sean looked at each other, defeat on their faces. "We're not sending anyone away," Sean said.

"Well, I should hope not," Reena replied, sinking down on the sofa beside Pam, patting her hand comfortingly.

"Chalk up another failure," Sean muttered to Andi.

Mike, who'd been quietly observing, got to his feet.

"Can we help load your gear?" Sean asked him.

"Please leave some of the food," Pam begged.

Mike laughed. "I'll leave it all, but I need to take back a couple of the coolers and other gear."

"I'll unload the coolers," Andi offered, and Mike followed her into the kitchen.

"Sorry," he apologized immediately, "I didn't know that bringing Mrs. Fleming over here would cause a problem."

"Reena can be very persuasive and stubborn, as you've observed. If you hadn't brought her, she would have gotten here somehow, just as Pam did."

"I'd be glad to sail them back. We can easily beat the storm by a couple of hours. I should have mentioned that to them."

"I know," Andi said as she stacked cans of soft drinks and packages of cold cuts on the counter. "By the way, thanks for the food. We'll have plenty for everyone."

"No problem," Mike said.

"As for sailing them back, even though Reena knows you can beat the storm, she's determined to stay for whatever reason. But Pam does look a little pale. It's probably best for her to wait until the bad weather passes. We can put off the test for another day," she added.

Mike picked up the empty cooler. "I can't say I hope you two work it out."

Andi frowned.

"Because I still want you to work with us at TSS."

"I have no idea how this will end," Andi said honestly.

The door opened. "Need me to take that?" Sean asked.

Mike handed over the cooler.

"I'll go ahead," Sean said.

"We're coming, too," Andi said quickly.

When the door closed, Mike commented, "He's ready to get rid of me."

Andi laughed. "No, he's just unsure of everything. We both are. Sometimes I have such hope, I feel so close to him, and then—" She gave Mike a sad little smile.

"Good luck," he said, "whatever happens. You know I want what's best for you."

"Thanks for your support, Mike."

They followed Sean out, and after Mike said goodbye to Reena and Pam, he and Andi headed for the dock.

"Don't forget the TSS offer still holds," Mike said.

"I won't."

They walked along in silence until Mike spoke again. "Did you know I'm opening offices in Europe?" He asked the question casually, but his eyes were intent on her face.

"No, I didn't," she answered thoughtfully.

"TSS will be offering crystal and linen from Ireland, woolens from Scotland, jewelry from Italy, and I'll need overseas buyers. Experienced retail people. Like you."

Andi stood on tiptoe and kissed his cheek. "You are a friend, Mike. Thanks. I'll keep my options open. Now the wind's coming up, so you better get under way."

They hurried toward the boat. "Do me one more favor," Andi asked. "Let Kevin know Pam's all right and will be coming home tomorrow. He might want to call Ed Ennis."

"Consider it done."

Sean stepped off the boat. "Stored your gear, Rossi."

"Thanks, Fleming."

There was an awkward silence before Sean extended his hand. "Thank you for the shortwave. And for taking care of Reena."

"Glad to do both." Mike stepped onto his boat. "And remember what I said, Andi."

Sean slipped his arm around Andi, bent over and asked, "And what was that?"

"Nothing important. Just business."

They watched Mike maneuver from the dock and head across the bay. The boat bobbed like a toy in the water. "I hope he'll be okay," Andi said.

"The guy's a good sailor, and he has tons of high tech equipment aboard. He knows what he's doing, Andi. Which is more than I can say for us."

"I guess we should have been firmer with Pam and Reena," Andi said, "but how do you tell your mother—"

"And your pregnant sister—"

"To get out? No, I think we were as firm as we could be. They'll leave tomorrow. Maybe."

"Until then, it's just like you said, babe, us against them." He smiled for a moment. "You know, I really like the sound of that."

9

REENA BUSTLED into the kitchen. "Do you have any soup, Andi? I think it might settle Pam's stomach."

"Nothing but vichyssoise."

"No, no. That won't do. Too creamy. How about a carbonated drink?"

"Champagne?"

"Andi, I'm being serious. She says she doesn't want anything, but I know better. Your sister isn't feeling well. We need to do something."

"If she says she doesn't want anything, she means it, Reena. The best solution would be to leave her alone."

"I can't possibly do that. There must be a carbonated drink around here."

"Mike brought some cola, but it's much too sweet." Andi checked out the supplies Mike had left. "Okay, here's a bottle of seltzer. It's still cold." Andi poured the drink into a glass and handed it to Reena.

"I'll sit with her while she sips it," the older woman declared as she hurried out of the kitchen.

Andi sighed. She was worried about Pam, too, but she knew her sister didn't like people hovering. Yet when Andi left the kitchen, she was surprised to find Reena acting the mother hen and Pam eating it up. They were seated on the sofa, engaged in intimate conversation.

"I like old-fashioned names like Rebecca and Sarah and Nathaniel," Pam was saying. "Kevin is a little more modern, so we really haven't agreed."

"We had such a hard time with my son's name. I wanted him to be called Scott—my maiden name— but my husband was stuck on Sean. I thought it sounded too Irish."

Sean came down the stairs. "It not only sounds Irish, it *is* Irish, Mother. And so was Dad's family." That stopped Reena temporarily, and Sean turned his attention to Andi. "I've closed and fastened all the shutters on the upper level. The wind is getting stronger by the minute. Maybe we should check out-side—pull the canoe onto dry land and bring in the deck chairs."

Andi nodded. It sounded as if Sean wanted to get out of the house as much as she did. "Will you two be all right?" she asked.

Pam and Reena weren't listening. Instead, they were deep in conversation. This time the subject was breast-feeding.

Andi slipped outside, where Sean was waiting on the porch. "I don't think they'll even know we've gone. But I am a little worried about Pam. I just hope the baby doesn't decide to be born—"

"There's no way it's going to happen," Sean said with a laugh. "Reena, the storm and a baby—all in one night! The fates wouldn't be that unkind."

"You're right," Andi said hopefully.

The waves in the usually quiet bay pounded against the shore, and the wind swirled, twisting the limbs of the pine trees. The damp, fresh scent of rain was in the air, mingling with the salty smell of the sea, which was dark blue, almost black, beneath the whitecaps. The sky had darkened, and huge gray clouds blocked the sun. It was as if night had descended in the middle of the afternoon.

Andi was exhilarated by the storm, which was building dangerously but somehow didn't seem threatening to her. For the first time in days, she felt free. She looked at Sean. His face was alive with excitement.

"Isn't this great?" he shouted above the wind. "There's something wild in the air before a storm. It's like this everywhere in the world. It's always fascinated me." Far away, thunder rolled and echoed across the sea.

"Me, too," Andi cried. She took his hand, and they headed for the shoreline, their feet digging deeply in the sand.

As they held onto each other at the water's edge, the waves splashed over their legs, the wind whipped their hair around their faces, and foaming ocean spray left their skin damp and salty.

Suddenly Sean picked Andi up and whirled her around. She laughed out loud, and the sound of her laughter was caught by the breeze and blown out to sea. He said something to her, but his words, too, were blown away.

He set her on her feet, and she leaned against him, still laughing. "I'm so dizzy, I feel drunk."

"I'm feeling a little crazy myself." Still holding her tightly against him, Sean put one hand under her chin and tilted her face upward. He tried to smooth her hair away, but the wind kept whipping it back wildly.

"This is like old times," he said, "the two of us, laughing, acting crazy."

Her eyes locked on his, and she couldn't look away from the intensity in their smoky depths. She was drawn deeper into them as his lips captured hers and he kissed her passionately, as if something from the storm compelled him.

Andi was sure she could hear the pounding of her heart above the roar of the sea and the rumbling of thunder in the distance. His arms held her hard against him, and a wave broke high, splashing around their knees. They were caught for a moment in the current, but he set his feet apart in the sand and held her tightly. Desire swirled around her like the sea as his mouth covered hers, moist, demanding. She opened her lips to taste him as another wave broke, higher, and pulled them apart.

Andi hung onto him, pulse racing, voice ragged, barely audible above the storm. "This could be dangerous."

"The storm?"

"No, us kissing."

"I love danger," he said. "Don't you?"

Her smile admitted that she did. "But we can't forget the storm, Sean. We have to move the canoe up to the trees."

"You're right." He grabbed her arms, smiling broadly, and pulled her backward, out of the swirling water. "Into the pines we go!"

They dragged the canoe into the shelter of the trees. Pine needles covered the ground in swirls of golden brown. Andi caught Sean's suggestive look. Here they were, under the trees, cooled by breezes heavy with the scent of impending rain, in a perfect place for love.

A place she didn't need to be. Tearing her gaze from his, she said, "Let's stow the canoe and get out of here."

As she turned to walk away, he grabbed her arm. "Later."

"Later?"

"Much later," he answered as he took her in his arms and kissed her again. The feel of her, soft against him, the fragrance of her scent, all that he'd been missing was his again. Holding her tightly, he sank to his knees and pulled her down with him. The threatening storm with its roaring wind, slashing lightning and crashing sea only heightened the passion of the moment. She belonged in his arms, and he wasn't going to let her go.

Andi pulled her lips away from his. "This is crazy—"

"I know, and that's why it's so wonderful." He kissed her neck, licked the outline of her ear, exploring the tender pink inside with the tip of his tongue. He wanted to taste all of her, to touch every inch of her body. His need for her knew no bounds. It was as wide as the sea and as powerful as the wind.

"No fair, Sean," Andi said, pushing against him. "When you do that, I can't think."

"This isn't about thinking," he said as he buried his face against her soft shoulder. "It's about *doing*, about feeling, loving."

"But the storm—"

"The storm is raging inside us, babe."

She attempted one more objection. "But here? Now?" Already, it was too late to fight it. Her voice was filled with anticipation.

"Remember when I told you that pine needles made a great bed?" He barely got the sentence out for the loud pounding of blood in his ears and coursing through his veins. His senses were filled with her. Nothing mattered to him but Andi and being close to her.

He lowered her to the ground, pulled off her T-shirt, unhooked her bra and tossed it away so he could kiss her breasts and the hollow between. He cradled her head in his hands and looked at her. Eyes dark with need, lips parted, soft and waiting, she was all that he desired and more. He felt his heart turn over in his chest.

"How can you say we don't know each other, Andi? I know the best of you, all the secret, wonderful parts of you. I know the little mole above your breast . . ." He kissed the spot tenderly. "I know the sounds you make when you sleep, the way you look waking up, how your face shines like the stars when we make love. I know the secret smile on your lips when I come inside of you. No one else knows that smile, Andi. No one."

She slipped her arms under his shirt and ran her fingers along the smooth muscles. His warmth enveloped her, and his words were hypnotic.

"I know your loyalty," he said, "and your dedication and sense of right. Why do you think I fell in love with you?"

She stopped the movement of her hands on his body and looked into his eyes as he spoke.

"Listen to me, Andi," he said in a voice more serious than she expected. "That was a stupid question I asked before—about why we fell in love, why we married. I *know* why. It's because of all the things you are to me, because of what we mean to each other. Those things can't change. They never will."

His words washed over her like soft, sweet music. She felt as though her heart would burst with love as he touched her, stroked her, held her close. But his words were the magic tonic. They made her spirit soar. She gave a sigh of acquiescence.

"I love the sound you make when you're happy."

"More than happy," she corrected. "Ecstatic."

"It's an impossible sound to duplicate," he said. "Kind of a moan-sigh. It happens when I touch your breasts . . ." He kissed each nipple gently. "And when I touch you here . . ." His hand drifted along her thigh. "And here." He slipped his fingers inside her panties.

Andi tried to keep the sound from escaping her lips.

"Go ahead, Andi, let me hear you. Talk to me, babe." His hands moved across her body, and as she let out a deep sigh, Sean found himself crying out, too. "Oh, Andi, I want you so much. I want to make love to you and take us both to places we've never been."

With shaking hands, she pulled his shirt over his head and helped him out of his running shorts.

Their naked bodies met, moist, slick and hot. Lightning cracked in the sky above them, and the sound of thunder shattered the day. She opened her mouth under his, tasted him, touched his tongue with hers and drifted into a kiss that she wished would never end.

"I know the best part of you, Andi. I know your heart," he whispered.

Above them, the pine trees swirled in the wind, the branches creating a tinny sound as the needles slapped against each other. Below them, their scattered clothes formed a soft bed on fallen pine needles.

She gazed at him, her eyes bright with tears. They were tears of love, tears of desire, tears of need. She longed to be part of him, to melt into him. In a powerful, jolting moment everything disappeared—the wind in the pines, the sound of the sea, the flashes of lightning in the sky. There was nothing but Sean and her aching need for him.

He twined his hands in her hair and locked his eyes on hers, loving her with his gaze as he loved her with his body. She felt as if they were joined not just where their bodies touched, but in their hearts and souls. Everywhere, they were one. His breath was hers, her heartbeat his. The pounding of his blood flowed inside her. She closed her eyes and gave herself to the moment.

They moved together as if by magic, each giving, each taking. The need inside her became a twisting coil of pleasure, so intense that every fiber of her being was immersed in the sensation. Her skin was hot and tight, damp with perspiration. Her heart was racing crazily and her breath came in short gasps. And deep within her a wave of sensual bliss was building, spiraling, intense and rapturous.

He watched the emotions sweep across her face and heard the strong sounds that accompanied them, sounds of yearning, striving, joy and—at last—surrender to passion. He was on that journey with her.

Her emotions were his. Her pleasure stoked the fires of his passion. The pressure built inside him, and the need became all encompassing. Still, he held back, waiting for her release.

When she began to tremble beneath him and her cries became fierce, he called out her name as he exploded inside her with a passion as wild and thunderous as the storm.

Gasping, they held each other, delighting in the feel of their passion-damp bodies until their racing hearts slowed. Then they lay still, watching the lightning flash all around them, until Andi began to squirm.

"What's the matter?" he asked.

"Pine needles, that's what."

He laughed. "They looked soft."

"Last time you saw them, you were on the roof. They probably did look soft from there. Down here, they're not so comfortable."

"You didn't complain while we were . . ."

"Making love," she finished. "I didn't feel them then. I only felt you." She leaned over and kissed him.

He hugged her close and whispered, "How can I ever let you go? I love you, Andi. I always will."

She kissed him again, thoroughly, as though she could never get enough of him. He kissed her back, and his mouth against hers was hot, sweet and delicious. "I love you, too. I want this marriage to work— more than anything, Sean."

"It will," he promised.

He pulled her on top of him, brushed the pine needles off her back and then carefully rearranged their rumpled clothes for her to lie on. "Comfortable?"

"Mmm. Perfect." She snuggled close. "But not for long."

"What now?"

"It's raining, Sean."

"No, it's not." He lay still, waiting. "That's just moisture on the wind." As soon as he spoke, a big raindrop splattered on his face, and then another and another.

"Damn. I was hoping we could spend the afternoon here."

"At least the rain held off long enough for us to make love." Andi rolled over, pulling the clothes out from under her.

"Why bother to dress?" he asked lazily. "We're only going to get wet."

"I can just see your mother as we come bounding up on the front porch, naked."

"Might be good for her," he answered as he pulled on his shorts. "One thing's for sure, we have to get them off this island. All we need is time—"

Andi held up her hand. "I thought I heard someone calling us."

He listened for a moment. "Nothing but wind and rain."

"Must've been my imagination," Andi said as she pulled her T-shirt over her head.

"Or a guilty conscience for romping naked in the woods." He pulled a few pine needles from her hair. "Let me dispose of the incriminating evidence."

Drenched and laughing, they did their best to straighten their clothes and, holding hands, ran through the trees and across the beach with the rain pounding down on them.

"We're behaving like naughty children," Andi cried.

"Good for us." Sean squinted through the rain. "Is that Reena on the porch—with a lantern? It's a wonder she didn't track us down in the woods."

Suddenly Andi was alarmed. "Something's the matter."

Reena met them at the bottom of the porch steps. "Where have you been?" she demanded angrily, oblivious of the rain. "We have to get Pam off this island, and do it now."

"What—" Andi began.

"The baby's coming!"

ANDI TORE into the living room where Pam was lying on the sofa, her face a grimace of pain and fear. Andi knelt beside her. "Pam, tell me the baby's not coming. It can't. *You* can't. Most of all, *we* can't deliver a baby!"

"Sorry, Sis, but it's coming. The contractions are—" she drew in her breath sharply and let it out "—just the way they described them in my prenatal class."

"No, no. They were wrong. You're wrong." Andi gripped Pam's hand with all her strength. "I know what's happened—it's false labor!"

Another pain hit. "Just false labor," she assured Pam, patting her hand again. Andi knew she was wrong, but she refused to give up the idea. The other possibility was unacceptable.

Pam pulled her hand away. "Come into the real world, Andi," she said. "This baby's not going to wait."

"Don't worry," Sean said, frantically fiddling with the dials on the shortwave. "It'll be okay."

Everyone turned to watch him, and he smiled encouragingly, the radio to his ear. Nothing happened, and Sean realized he didn't know a damn thing about shortwaves, broken or not. Suddenly, he was startled by loud bursts of static. "It's working, it's working," he shouted, heading toward the kitchen. "I'll just go in here, and call for help. Don't worry. I'll get through," he shouted.

Andi thought he sounded like a superhero from the comics, and she didn't believe his assurance for a minute. But at least he was doing something, not just denying reality. Reena moved constantly in nervous anxiety as thunder crashed overhead and shook the cabin in its intensity.

"I hope Sean can get through to the mainland," she said, raising her voice above the sound of the rain, which was now driving against the windows in sheets.

"I'm sure he can," Andi replied, "now that we have a good radio." Even as she uttered the brave words, her eyes and Reena's met. It would have been difficult for her to say who was the most worried.

Sean appeared briefly at the kitchen door. His voice was unnaturally calm as he asked, "Andi, could you come here for a second, please?"

Pam's face contracted in another spasm of pain, and she clung to Andi's hand until it passed. Then she smiled wanly. "I've decided this natural childbirth is for the birds. Got any drugs on you?"

"They won't be necessary," Andi said cheerfully. "Because your baby isn't going to be born here. It's going to be born in a hospital with nurses and doctors taking care of you and with your husband standing by. That's final," Andi said confidently. Then she summoned Reena, and replaced her own hand with the older woman's.

"There," she said, as if to prove everything was all right as long as someone was holding Pam's hand. "I'll go into the kitchen for a moment."

She shot out of the room and through the kitchen door. "What is it? Tell me you've roused someone."

"Yes and no. The reception is awful, but I got through. Frankly, I was damned surprised when I heard a voice answering me."

"Is someone coming? What did he say?"

"He said there was a small craft warning, and the Coast Guard can't get out of Clarion harbor. They're going to see if the emergency service can get a chopper in the air—"

Just then the cabin was shaken by a blast of wind. Andi's face crumpled in despair. "In this storm?"

Sean took her in his arms. "It's going to be okay," he soothed.

She clung to him, trying to fight overwhelming feelings of helplessness and terror. "She can't have the baby here. She could die. It could die."

His voice was determined, if grim. "Andi, the baby's going to be born on Pawlie's Island, and soon. It's out of our hands, and we'll have to handle it."

"No, we can't! Try the radio again. Call emergency or try SOS. What about Mayday? Isn't that the distress signal for emergencies at sea? Well, this is an emergency! Dial the number for the army, the navy— the marines!"

Sean tried not to laugh. "I'll do what I can, Andi, but in the end we'll have to deliver this baby."

"No," she repeated. "I've never even seen a baby being born."

"I have," he said. "In Zaire and Bosnia and Lebanon. Under much worse conditions than this." He took her face in his hands. "We're a team. If we have to do it, we will. Pam and her baby will be all right. Trust me."

She touched his face with her fingertips. "If I ever wanted to trust you, it's now. But I hope you're wrong about the baby."

Reena appeared in the door, looking totally distraught. "What are you two doing? This isn't the time for fooling around. Sean, get on that shortwave."

"I've been on it, Reena," he said calmly. "Until the storm lifts, they can't get help to us."

Reena's voice was tight. "Then get the paramedics on that thing—"

"I've got a call in to them."

"Good," she said, "because her water's broken. This baby is coming soon."

"No, it's not," Andi said adamantly. "I won't let it!" She dashed into the living room.

Reena looked at Sean and shrugged her shoulders. "Your wife's in for a surprise."

"We're all in for some tough work, Mom."

Reena rolled up her sleeves and peered into the stove. "The fire's still going, but we need more wood. I'll start boiling water—" She looked at him with a bewildered laugh. "Well, that's what they do in the movies."

Sean gave her a quick hug. She suddenly seemed small and fragile in his arms, and he felt very protective of her. "They do it because it's necessary, Mom, so let's get to work. I'm glad you're here," he added.

He could see her fight back the tears. "It's been a long time since I had a baby, but I remember a few things. Pam's brave, Andi's smart, I've got lots of guts. We're quite a trio of dames."

"The best," he said. "Now let's get this show on the road."

Sean added wood to the fire, and while Reena boiled water, he tried the shortwave again, getting nothing but static. He had put an emergency medical call out. All he could do was wait for a response.

Once she had two pots of water boiling, Reena returned to the living room. Sean put aside the radio long enough to find a sharp knife and pair of scissors in a kitchen drawer. He dropped them into a pot. Then he untied his laces and pulled them out of his running shoes. Not ideal, but they'd do for tying off the umbilical cord. If it came to that. And it sure as hell looked like it would.

He opened the kitchen door and looked. Pam was ensconced on what Sean realized was a sofa bed. Andi and Reena had opened it for her and were doing their best to make her comfortable. Reena glanced up, met his eyes and smiled, a brave but shaky look that proved her courage and compassion at a time when, clearly, she was petrified.

Andi was equally brave and efficient—on the outside. She wasn't letting her fear show. If there was ever a test, not of their marriage, but of will and determi-

nation, this was it—and Sean was determined he
would pass.

Back at the shortwave, he punched send and repeated his earlier call. "SOS, SOS, patch me in at once
to emergency medical on the mainland. Pawlie's Island calling. SOS, SOS . . ."

"I'M SORRY, Andi," Pam said after a contraction
ended.

"About having the baby when I told you not to?"
Andi questioned. "Don't worry. I'm getting used to
the idea."

"No, I'm talking about the store, about arguing
with you and chasing you guys over here—"

"Are you kidding? I don't care about the store.
Open a chain of them, if you want. Just so you and this
baby are safe. Nothing else matters," she said fiercely.

Pam managed a smile. "Everything else seems
pretty silly, doesn't it?"

"It sure does." Andi wiped Pam's damp brow. She
wished she could do more, at least assure her sister
that everything would be all right, but she was still
worried something might go wrong. "I wish Kevin
was here with us," she admitted.

"Me, too, but he'd have fallen apart already. That's
how he is. But your man is different. Sean's so cool.
He's taken charge. I was wrong when I said he wasn't
husband material. He's the best."

"He's used to hazardous duty," Andi joked. Pam
gave a little moan and squeezed Andi's hand tightly.
"Bad one?" she asked.

"The worst so far." Pam gasped.

"It's time for your breathing. Come on, Pam, I'll do it with you."

Pam took some short breaths, which ended in a tentative giggle. "This breathing thing is vastly overrated. Can't I have brandy instead?"

"Absolutely not," Reena said. "However, I think it's mandatory for the medical staff."

"There's a bottle on the bookcase," Andi directed.

"She's quite a woman," Pam whispered. "We've had some great talks. I really like her."

"I do, too," Andi murmured, "and I never thought I would."

She smiled her thanks at the brandy Reena handed her, and downed it in one swallow. It warmed her to the pit of her stomach but did nothing to quell her nervousness.

Reena pulled a chair up to the bed and sipped her drink, staring at her watch. "I don't know why I'm timing the contractions," she said with a shake of her head. "It's not as if we'll go rushing off to the hospital—"

"A helicopter could make it," Andi said staunchly.

"No way," Pam said. "This baby is coming before a copter gets off the pad."

"The Coast Guard could—"

"Or before a boat leaves the dock," Pam said just as another pain hit.

Andi held onto her hand and watched Pam try, unsuccessfully, to stifle a shriek. Her own forehead broke out in perspiration as she wiped Pam's face with one hand and held onto her with the other.

"It's going to be all right," Reena assured as she hovered over them. While Pam rode out the contraction, she added, "These circumstances aren't wonderful, but they could be worse. Women have babies in all sorts of places. You could be in a taxi—or at a fast-food restaurant."

To Andi's amazement, Pam managed a grin. "One baby, please, hold the lettuce and pickle. I wish it was that simple."

"Your baby will be very special," Reena added. "Born in the midst of this—this hurricane. It will just make him, or her, that much stronger."

"If she's a girl, let's name her Storm," Andi added.

"Or Tempest," Pam said. "Or maybe—" Her words were cut off by a scream she was unable to stem.

"Pant with me, Pam. Breathe!"

Sean stepped into the room and waited until Pam fell back, exhausted. "I had the paramedics on the shortwave—"

"Bring the radio over. Hurry, they'll tell us what to do," Andi cried.

"But I lost them—"

"No!" Andi was almost hysterical.

"Don't worry," he said calmly. "I have it all up here." He tapped his forehead.

"All the instructions for delivering a baby?" Andi was aghast. "I thought someone would be on the other end to talk us through it. I thought—"

"Sean will remember," Reena said in a proud voice. "If he can remember pages of a TV script, it'll be easy for him."

"Nothing to it," Sean said. "Just trust Dr. Fleming."

"What choice do I have?" Pam groaned. "You're the only show in town."

"And the best, honey," he replied. "When the time comes . . ."

"It's getting close," Pam moaned.

"Reena, you come up here and hold her shoulders. Try to get her comfortable," Sean advised. "Someone needs to catch the baby. That should be you, Andi."

"Me?" Andi was aghast.

"Yes," Pam agreed. "I want you to be the first person to hold my baby, Andi."

Andi swallowed hard. "Well...sure." When she let go of Pam's hand, she realized how hard she was trembling, and when she got to her feet, she had to hold on to Sean to keep from falling. As far as she was concerned, their marriage test had turned into a nightmare of epic proportions. But there was no escaping now. She tried to stand on her own.

Sean gave her a comforting pat and then a little push toward the kitchen. "Wash your hands first," he said in a gentle but firm voice.

Andi did as she was told, trying to stall but realizing as she heard her sister's moans that she couldn't stop the inevitable. She returned to the room.

"As soon as you see the baby's head, support it, but let Pam do the work," Sean told her.

Andi took her place at the end of the bed with trepidation. The look she gave Sean said she wasn't up to the job.

"Reena will coach you," he said. "She's a pro." He smiled at Andi and winked at his mother. Reena had been unconscious when he was born and didn't remember a thing. Sean knew that. But as long as Andi—and Pam—weren't aware of it, they'd be okay.

"My mouth's so dry," Pam croaked. "Could I have a sip of water?"

"I'll get it!" Andi shot into the kitchen.

Sean sat opposite his mother, holding Pam's hand.

She looked at him, her face pale and worried. "You're a good man, Sean. Sorry I messed things up for you and Andi. I want you to make it, and I want you both—and Reena—to be a part of my baby's life."

Sean kissed her lightly on the forehead. "I've never had a sister and I've never been an uncle. I'm looking forward to both."

Pam tried to answer but instead writhed in pain. "This is bad, Sean! I think it's coming. I feel the baby pushing, pushing—"

Andi charged in from the kitchen, her face ashen, her eyes wide with fright. The cup of water sloshed as she ran to Pam.

Sean took the cup from her hand and held it to Pam's lips.

She wet her lips and then pushed it away. "Sean—"

"I know," he said. "We're having a baby," he told Andi, motioning for her to take her place. "And we're having it now."

There was a blinding crash of lightning followed by an answering roll of thunder. Andi crouched beside her sister, rearranged the sheet draping Pam's legs and shot a look at Sean.

He was talking to Pam, breathing with her, coaching her, his voice slow, even and filled with confidence.

"Easy, easy. This baby knows how to be born, honey. Just go with the flow, relax and breathe."

Andi closed her eyes, wishing she could blot out Pam's cries, the roar of the storm and the sound of her own frantic heartbeat. But she was helpless and ineffectual, nowhere near as calm and strong as Sean.

This was a Sean she'd never seen, a man under pressure, who could handle what really counted in life. She believed she'd known him; she'd called him selfish and careless. Now she realized she hadn't known him at all. Not until tonight.

Pam's cries were intense, her breathing labored and harsh. "This is it," Sean said. "Get ready, Andi. Just hold onto that baby."

10

LONG AFTER MIDNIGHT, Andi and Sean were in the kitchen—exhausted, exalted and functioning on pure adrenaline.

Andi gazed in loving wonder at the infant sleeping in her arms. She would remember this as the worst—and best—night of her life. No matter what the future held for her, how many children she might have, she would always feel a mystical bonding with this very special baby.

"I'm in love," she said, "totally and completely. He's wonderful."

"Love at first sight does happen," Sean reminded her softly. "I can vouch for that."

"So can I," Andi said. But her thoughts were on the baby. "Look at him, Sean. He's the most beautiful baby in the world."

Sean leaned over her shoulder and examined the little pink bundle. "Actually he looks a little like—what are those dogs with the pinched faces? Pekingese. He looks like one of those to me."

"He does not," she protested.

"He's kind of wrinkled and red."

"Sean—"

"But as babies go, he's beautiful, I guess."

"Look at his little nose. So darling. And his perfect little ears."

"Mmm," was Sean's noncommittal reply.

She decided not to mention the baby's rather puffy eyes. "And the fingers. Just look. They're perfect. So are his toes."

"They're absolutely—beautiful," Sean said with a laugh. "No, Andi, I mean it," he added when she gave him a dirty glance. "He's a great little kid."

She looked at him with a smile. "We did it."

"We sure did, babe." He wrapped his arms around both of them. "We're a hell of a team when we need to be."

Andi leaned against him. She was as exhausted as he was, but her mind couldn't stop working. "I'm still worried," she admitted. "Pam and the baby need medical care—"

"As soon as the storm lets up, I'll get on the short-wave. By daylight we'll have transportation to the mainland. I guarantee."

"I trust you," she said immediately. "You promised that we could deliver this baby, and we did. You were wonderful—and so was Reena."

"She'd like to hear that from you. Now hand him over. It's my turn to hold this beautiful baby."

"No fair. I've only had him a few minutes," she argued.

"That's all each of us gets. Pam'll be waking up soon, and I have a feeling she'll want him back. Now hand over my nephew."

Reluctantly, she gave him the baby.

"This guy will always be special to me," Sean said, gently touching the baby's face.

Sean was right, she thought. The baby was special to both of them. He'd created a bond between her and

Sean that hadn't existed before, one that would last forever. No matter what happened, that bond would remain. And they would never forget this night.

As she watched Sean cradle the baby in his big hands, Andi's heart gave a lurch. In spite of his teasing remarks, she could see that her husband was totally transfixed by his little nephew. The two made a wonderful picture, the tiny pink baby, sleeping peacefully, and the big man, tired-looking, wearing stained clothes, his hair tousled and his eyes darkly shadowed, his face covered by a three-day growth of beard.

Certainly, this Sean looked nothing like the sophisticated and daring foreign correspondent she'd fallen in love with. Instead, he seemed sensitive, vulnerable and far more likable. His fans would probably say he looked like hell, but to Andi he was more beautiful than he'd ever been. Especially on the inside. She felt a surge of pride and a surprising quickening of tears in her eyes.

Sean was babbling to the baby, making unintelligible noises. After a while, he began to talk in a more adult way. "I think he understands real words better than baby talk. Hey, little fellow. How're you doing?" Sean watched, mesmerized, as the baby opened and closed his eyes.

"I think he's listening," Andi said.

"Of course he is. And look at that. He can put his finger in his mouth."

"Can ordinary babies do that?" Andi realized she knew as little as Sean about the subject.

"I'm sure they can't. This one's a genius. You're brilliant . . . Hey, what do we call the kid? Pam needs to name him."

"She's probably waiting until they get home and Kevin can have some input."

Reena appeared in the doorway. "Pam's awake and wants her baby." She held out her arms. "I'll take him to her."

"Nope," Sean argued. "We can't keep passing him around like a trophy. I'll take him. Come on, little fellow. Let's go see your mom."

Reena shrugged and moved aside. "Well, don't let me hold you up," she said with an understanding smile.

"I may be gone a little while," Sean told her, "so would you two make some coffee? We need to stay wired in case Pam or the baby needs us. Here we go, kid."

Reena rolled her eyes. "A new side of my son emerges."

"This has been quite a night for all of us," Andi said. "I sure have a new perspective on life."

"A new baby. A new day." Reena glanced at her watch. "Just a few more hours until sunrise."

"And a new beginning," Andi said. She took a deep breath. "Reena, I want to apologize for the way I've acted. I wasn't very gracious when you came to Pawlie's, and before that, when I didn't visit you—" She paused. "This is so awkward."

"I know what you mean, because I feel the same way," Reena admitted as she measured coffee. "I shouldn't have come charging over here after you and Sean. I knew you wanted to be alone. But I felt so left out." She gave a relieved sigh. "There, I've said it. Left out of my son's life. I blamed you for that, which was wrong. You hardly saw more of him than I did when you two were abroad."

Andi laughed. "That's true, but he's back now, and we both have to deal with him—and with each other."

Reena's face was devoid of makeup; she'd chewed off her lipstick long ago, and Andi could see—even by the light of a kerosene lamp—the lines her mother-in-law usually tried to hide. And for the first time, Reena seemed real to her, and very human.

Andi hugged her tightly. "You were wonderful tonight, Reena. Our own mother couldn't have done more." With those last words, Andi's voice cracked with emotion.

Reena's tired face softened. "Thanks for saying that. Pam needed someone tonight, and I guess I was needy, too." She poured Andi and herself coffee and sank down in a chair at the table. Andi could see that she wanted to unburden herself.

"After my husband's death, when Sean went off to school, I realized I didn't have much of a life. I filled my hours, but I needed more."

Andi didn't know how to respond. She and Reena had never talked openly or honestly.

"After all these years, I finally understand that what I missed most was a family. That's why I made the decision," she added, "to move to Clarion."

Andi looked up, startled.

"So I can help Pam with the baby and the store."

"You're moving to Clarion?" Andi asked.

"I certainly am. Do you disapprove?"

"Of course not. I'm stunned," she replied. "But now that I think about it . . ."

"Yes?" Reena asked.

Andi smiled broadly. "It's a wonderful idea. You'll be fantastic with the baby—and with the store."

Reena sipped her coffee. "I won't make it a permanent move until I see how things work out, but I believe I can help, don't you?" She went on before Andi had a chance to agree. "Pam and I get along well, and I've run the hospital auxiliary shop for years. I'm a good saleswoman."

Andi hid a smile. This was the old Reena. "You'll be great. You have such taste and style," Andi said, leaning over to kiss the older woman's cheek. "Thanks. It's the perfect solution for us all."

Reena's eyes glazed with tears. "Don't thank me. I should be thanking you and Pam for sharing your family with me."

"No, Reena, we owe you. Without you, we'd have been in trouble."

"Nonsense. You and Sean would have done just fine. You're a good team."

"That's what I keep telling her." Sean joined them in the kitchen and put an arm around each of them. "So, how're the two most important women in my life?"

"We're fine, but how's the really important woman—and her baby?"

"Sleeping—and sleeping," he replied. "I decided it was safe to slip away for some coffee."

"You two have coffee. I'll sit with Pam," Reena volunteered.

"Mom, she'll be fine," Sean replied.

"But she might wake up and need something. I think it's a good idea for someone to always be there with her and the baby, especially this soon after the birth. I'll just go and check things out . . ." Before she finished speaking, she was through the door and on her way.

Sean shrugged. "Instant grandmother."

"You don't know the half of it," Andi said. "Did she tell you she's moving to Clarion to help Pam out?"

"Nah, you're kidding."

"That's what she says." Andi poured a cup of coffee for Sean.

"Thanks." He took a sip. "Actually, it's not a bad idea. Mother's being there would certainly take the pressure off." He rubbed his stubbled chin thoughtfully. "Not just off Pam, but you, too. Yep, I like the idea. I like it a lot." He dropped a kiss on Andi's forehead. "How about some breakfast, babe? Or should I give it a try, scramble up some eggs?"

"No," Andi said quickly. "We've seen you at the stove. I'll fix something."

"Great, because I'm starved. The storm has almost blown itself out. I'm going to try the shortwave again."

Andi realized that the wind had died, and the rain had become a soft murmur beating against the windows. Just as the storm had quietened, so had the emotions of the house. It was a relief to be doing something ordinary like slicing bread and cutting cheese while Sean toyed with the radio.

"Clarion, Clarion," he called, "come in, emergency." He'd patched in that call a dozen times, but now that the weather was clearing, he expected a response.

Andi kept working, her back to Sean, praying that he'd get through. If not, they'd have to wait for Ed Ennis to appear. She couldn't bear to think of Pam and the baby crowded into Ed's tiny lobster boat. While her mind raced, Sean's hands kept busy. Then a voice came across the static.

"Pawlie's, this is Clarion Med Evac. What is your emergency? Over."

Andi turned toward Sean, listening intently. His voice was calm and precise. It was his TV voice, she thought.

"This is Pawlie's, Clarion. We have a mother and her newborn who need medical care. Please send a chopper ASAP. Do you copy?"

"We read you loud and clear, Pawlie's. Can you advise a landing site? Over."

Sean glanced at Andi. "The beach?" he mouthed.

"The tide's too high. And they'll never be able to land with all those rocks." Then it came to her. "The meadow!"

Sean smiled. "Clarion, we have a landing site . . ."

"THE SUN'S almost up. Let's get going," Andi said.

"Look again, Andi. It's still dark. Give the sun a little time," Sean said.

Pam breathed a sigh and sat back, the baby cuddled in her arms. "Good idea. We'll have a chance to talk, and I have lots to say."

"You need to conserve your strength," Andi cautioned. "We can talk later."

"Listen, big sister, I've earned the right to say whatever I want—at least for today." Pam's stubbornness suddenly surfaced, baby notwithstanding. "I have an important announcement, and I want everyone to pay attention."

"We're all listening," Reena declared.

Pam smiled her thanks. "This is about names. I've decided on my baby's name." She paused dramatically. "And I know that Kevin will go along with me. We had some disagreements before, but he'll like this name as much as I do. For different reasons. He'll like it because it's such a great boy's name..."

"Come on, Sis, don't keep us in suspense," Andi urged.

"And I'll like it," Pam continued, paying no attention to Andi, "because of what it means to me—and to everyone who got through the night with me."

"Pam," Andi said, exasperated.

"Especially Reena Scott Fleming, the honorary grandmother of my son, whose name will be—Scott."

Reena made no attempt to fight tears, which she brushed away with the back of her hand. "Oh, Pam, I'm so thrilled." She had a sudden afterthought. "But are you sure Kevin will agree?"

"Absolutely. Besides, Kevin can choose a middle name." She giggled. "What a kick. Kevin doesn't even know he's a daddy yet."

"Yes, he does," Sean corrected. "I asked the medical guys to call him. He knows you and the baby are okay. He'll be there to meet you." Sean grinned. "But I didn't tell them what kind of baby you had. Thought you guys would like to convey that news yourselves."

"Thanks, Sean," Pam said, smiling at the baby nestled next to her. "Scott and I will let Daddy know." She looked up. "Do you think Kevin'll know just by looking at him?"

"Definitely," Andi said. "He's all boy."

Reena had gone to the back door and was looking out over the pine trees. "There's the sun," she declared. "Time to go!"

Andi's eyes met Sean's. She could read the reaction in his face and knew he was thinking what she was— everything was coming to an end.

"I CAN WALK," Pam argued.

"You just had a baby," Andi said.

"So? One of my friends walked back from the delivery room after her baby was born."

"That's just wonderful, Pam," Reena put in. "But it's also ridiculous. Besides, you weren't in a delivery room. You were in the living room of a cabin on a remote island with three untrained people and no medicine. After that, you don't walk. My son carries you."

Sean had already scooped Pam's blanket-wrapped body into his arms.

Andi carefully held Scott, who'd been diapered in a hand towel, then wrapped in a blanket. Reena carried another blanket, a bottle of seltzer and a couple of extra towel diapers. In single file, the little party stepped onto the porch.

Andi paused at the top of the stairs and inhaled the crisp, clean air. It was a glorious day, with the sun glistening through a clear blue sky and shattering into diamond shards that skipped across the waves.

Softly, Andi whispered, "It's your first day on earth, Scott. Welcome to the world, and may every day you live be this perfect."

"That's a nice thought," Sean whispered to her. "I wish the same for us."

Their eyes held for a moment over the heads of little Scott and his mother. Then it was time for the trek to the meadow.

Although the storm had passed, leaving clear skies behind, waves still pounded the shore, and the beach was almost obliterated by high tide. Because of the rocks, it wasn't possible to get to the meadow along the shore.

They made their way through the pine forest, following the shortcut Sean had found on his run. He threw a look Andi's way as they circled the cozy spot where they'd made love. She blushed and covered Scott's face. "Don't look, baby. You're too young."

She could hear Sean's laughter and the questions that followed from Pam, which he fended off easily.

As they cleared the pines, they moved more carefully. There was no path, and Andi skirted the rocks, holding the tiny bundle tightly in her arms and following the broad back of her husband while Reena brought up the rear.

Glancing over her shoulder, Andi saw Reena's face set fiercely as she moved with difficulty but determination. Her always chic mother-in-law hadn't bothered to apply makeup, her hair was windblown, and her once-immaculate sailing outfit was stained and wrinkled. What a group, Andi thought, bedraggled, dirty and tired.

They approached a very rocky section and Sean paused, shifting Pam in his arms.

"Put me down for a while so you can rest," she said.

"Not a chance," he told her. "If I put you down, I'd never be able to pick you up again!"

They all laughed, but Andi imagined that he was telling the truth. She could see the strain of his back and shoulder muscles through his T-shirt.

"That's okay," Pam said. "I can walk the rest of the way."

"Pam, don't you dare—" Andi began.

"Just kidding, but maybe I can crawl."

Reena caught up with them and squared her shoulders mightily. "Andi and I can make a basket with our arms and carry her."

"Give me a break," Pam said. "I'll stay where I am, thanks."

"It won't be long," Sean told them. "I can hear the helicopter. Double-time, gang." He shifted Pam again and took a deep breath. "We're almost there."

THEY CRESTED the hill and headed toward the meadow, an almost perfect circle of green grasses and colorful wildflowers sparkling in the early morning dew. Andi looked up. The helicopter appeared above the tree line, the noise of its rotors a deafening roar. Scott let out a whimper that swelled into a squall. Andi turned her back to the chopper as it landed, protecting the baby from the tornado of leaves and dirt swirling in the air.

The aircraft touched down, and two young men in khaki uniforms jumped out, bending over to stay well below the whirling blades. "There's enough room for you to ride beside your wife," one of the men shouted at Sean.

"She's not my wife. Her sister will go with her."

Andi nodded in agreement. She'd planned to accompany Pam. Someone had to go, and why not her closest relative?

"My sister has other plans," Pam announced as she took the baby from Andi and settled him in her arms. His crying stopped almost immediately. "She's not going with us."

"But Pam, someone has to," Andi said, "and I'm family—"

"After tonight, we're all family," Pam said. "Including Reena, who'll ride with us in the helicopter."

Reena stepped forward. "I didn't trail after you for exercise. Pam and I worked this out and decided that you and Sean deserve to get back to your lives without us."

"But—" Andi said.

"So I'm going with Pam. Now, give me that precious baby while you get into this machine, Pam," Reena commanded, "and let's get this show on the road."

"She needs me," Andi said weakly.

"She needs someone," Reena said. "That someone might as well be me until she gets home. Then she'll have Kevin."

Nodding in agreement, Pam passed the baby to Reena, kissed Andi and Sean and let herself be lifted into the helicopter.

"As for you two," Reena added, "from what I can tell, you need each other." Lovingly, she transferred the baby again, this time into his mother's waiting arms. "Now, young man," she ordered the pilot, "help me up into this thing."

Moments later, everyone was settled, the heavy doors were closed, and the rotors beat the air frantically as the copter lifted. Andi and Sean clung together and watched it hover, rise and shoot up into the clear blue sky. Then they watched it soar away toward the mainland.

Andi felt drained and—in a strange way—lost. The crisis was over, the emergency passed. Everything was back to normal. Only she didn't quite know what normal was. Besides that, the world around them seemed in flux, too, totally silent, not the sound of a bird or the chirp of a cricket. Even the usually active bees seemed to have been stunned into silence. She and Sean were very much alone, and for a moment she felt empty.

Then he gave her a tired hug, and she felt much better. The noises of the world returned.

"Can you make it back to the cabin, babe?"

"If you're beside me." She took his hand. "I could sleep for a week."

"For a day, at least, and then we have to talk, Andi. The time has come."

LATE IN THE afternoon, Andi awoke, stretched and opened her eyes. "You were watching me sleep," she said to Sean. "No fair."

"Don't you remember?"

"Remember what?" she asked.

"I always used to watch you sleep in the old days. I'd get back from an assignment, come to the hotel in the middle of the night, crawl into bed and watch you sleep before waking you up so we could make love."

"You never told me."

"Of course I did. You just forgot."

"Maybe I was embarrassed."

"Maybe. Are you embarrassed now?"

"No," she said. "I'm flattered. I can't imagine I look too great after sleeping for twelve hours."

"You look wonderful," he told her. His head was propped on his hand, his body turned toward hers on the bed. Languidly, he pushed a tendril of hair from her face. "This test of yours turned out to be more than either of us expected."

"It was a silly idea," she said regretfully.

"No, it wasn't," he disagreed. "The test got us here to Pawlie's, it got us talking—"

"It certainly taught me a lot about you," she said seriously.

"That I fall off roofs, turn over canoes and make the world's worst bouillabaisse?" He gave a wry twist to his mouth, remembering. "All failing grades."

"Maybe," she admitted, "but I learned a few other things. That you're strong and brave. You held us together, Sean, when the baby was born."

"I doubt that. Women are always stronger than men."

"You were the glue that made us a team," she insisted. "You have great strength of character, Sean Fleming. I never knew that before." She smiled impishly. "In fact, I'm amazed."

He leaned forward and kissed her nose. "What happened to those negative adjectives like careless and selfish?"

"I'm sure you still have traces of them—"

"Oh?"

"But they've been wiped out by your better qualities. Besides, people can change. Not only you, but me."

"You had me nailed pretty good originally, babe. That's when you'd never seen me under fire, to use a cliché. I'm at my best in a crisis."

"I hope that doesn't mean we have to go through the rest of our lives in search of crises—so we can be a great team." She met his eyes directly. The afternoon sun sliced warmly across them, but in spite of that, Andi felt the prickle of a chill up her spine. What kind of team were they? In the day-to-day routine of life, could they make it?

She didn't know the answer to that question.

Sean watched her for a moment as the doubts flickered through her mind. Then he rolled to the side of the bed and sat there, feet on the floor, head resting in his hands. The room was quiet except for the nervous pounding of her heart as she watched him.

"I guess this is it, Andi," he said finally. "The moment of truth when we decide about our lives—and our marriage."

Andi sat back against the headboard, her arms wrapped around her knees. "Let's not kid ourselves. One thing this test has taught me is to be realistic. I was living a fantasy back in Clarion, when I made my neat little list."

"We both had a lot to learn then."

"Well, we're never going to have a storybook marriage, that's for sure. We're never going to laugh and joke at seven in the morning as we cook breakfast to-gether—"

"Hell, we're never going to cook breakfast to-gether, no matter what time of day," he reminded her. "And I'm not ever going to be happy doing house-hold chores. I'm not a domestic guy, Andi."

"I know," she said. "But neither am I!"

"Then we'll hire a maid."

She kissed him. "I'm glad you said that."

"At least when we're in one place . . ."

"I'm still not going to run after you, tearing through life at your frenetic pace, never stopping to look—"

"At the tide pools," he finished for her. "Let's face it, Andi. I'm never going to be a shell collector," he said firmly.

"Obviously, we don't fit in the regular marriage mode."

He turned to look at her, his gray eyes sparkling. "That's it!"

"What?"

"We've been trying to fit into a normal marriage thing . . ."

"Yeah?"

"But we aren't a normal couple."

She nodded. "Agreed. Most couples don't spend their time chasing around the world . . ."

"And then landing on a deserted island . . ."

"Just in time to deliver a baby!" She tumbled for-ward, laughing, into his arms.

"Why do we have to follow anyone else's rules, babe? Why can't we have our marriage the way we want, with the two of us making up our own rules as we go along?"

"Why not? That's what we've done so far." She snuggled into his body. "But we never had a chance to depend on each other until now. Never had a crisis except what to order for dinner or what four-star hotel to check into."

"Not much of a marriage to that point," he admitted. "You were right to leave me in Europe. I didn't have a clue what marriage was all about."

"I felt I didn't have a place in your life."

"I felt like that, too," he told her.

"You felt alone?"

"Yes, closed out by you and your family. You made it clear who you were choosing—and it wasn't me."

"All that time, I thought you were angry. I never knew you were hurt."

"Just as you were," he added.

"If only we'd done more of this, just sitting and talking, instead of playing honeymoon games."

"No more games," he said, squeezing her hand. "I want to keep on talking—through the rest of our lives. So I've made a decision."

She looked up at him.

"I'm going to stay in the States, in Maine. I imagine there's a job out there for a New England anchorman." He added in a theatrical voice, "Today tragedy struck in Clarion, Maine, when two demented moose—" He looked down at Andi. "Or is it mooses—or meese?"

"Don't make fun of Maine," she said.

"No way. I'm going to love it since I plan to be living here."

"Oh, yeah?"

"Yeah. Do you have a better idea?"

"I sure do," she said. "Mike offered me a job as European buyer for TSS, based in London. I've decided to take it."

Sean leaned over her. "Rossi offered you a job overseas?"

"Yep."

"And you're going to take it?"

"Yep."

He fell back, holding her in his arms, laughing. "To think that Mike Rossi is turning out to be my best friend. Who would have thought it?"

"Who would have thought any of this?" she asked. "A baby born, a marriage saved—"

"And us taking off for Europe."

"But not yet. We have to get to know my nephew first."

"*Our* nephew. I'm going to get him a present as soon as we get back. Kids like those Power Rangers, don't they? But I'm old-fashioned. I think I'll get a fire truck. Or maybe a train set."

"Sean, he's only a day old."

"So? You're never too young for presents. Don't stop me from spoiling him, Andi."

She sighed. "One thing won't ever change. We'll still disagree frequently."

"And argue like crazy," he agreed.

"I'll gripe when you fly off to cover a story—"

"And I'll complain when you..." He starting laughing. "I'm sure I'll complain, but I don't even know what you'll be doing."

"Shopping for exotic import items..."

"Easy to complain about you running around,

poking into shops, taking precious time away from our marriage."

Andi began to laugh. "We definitely won't have a conventional marriage, will we?"

"Nope. But it'll be ours. The two of us against the world," he said fiercely, gathering her to him. "We've proven that our love is strong enough to make it work this time. We've been tested and tried on the field of battle."

"Sounds overly dramatic, like something on TV," she said.

"You're disagreeing with me," he cautioned her.

"You're right about that," she said, cuddling close, running her fingers through his tousled hair. She could hear the slow, rhythmic beat of his heart, feel his warmth and strength flowing through her.

"That's the way it's going to be—and I'm all for it," he said, giving her a big hug.

"But we still haven't resolved one issue," she told him.

He laughed. "I'm not surprised. What's the problem?"

"It's about babies. Scott's birth made me feel . . . well, loving and protective. I've decided having a baby isn't such a bad idea."

"And I've decided we're probably not ready yet."

She sighed. Another disagreement.

"Really, Andi, a baby is a hell of a lot of responsibility. You said that yourself, and you were right. We both need to be ready."

She pulled his face to hers and kissed him hard. "Whatever you say, husband . . ."

"Whatever I say?" he questioned.

"At least for today—or for this afternoon—or the next hour."

He returned the kiss, deeply, thoroughly, the first kiss of their new life together. He let his lips drift to her neck, her hairline, her ear. "What if your husband says he'd like to try a little love in the afternoon. Not on a table. Or in a chair..."

"Not on the beach or in the woods."

"But on a bed. This bed—our bed."

She smiled up at him. "This time I agree—totally," she said, her heart filled with love.

Epilogue

London, England
Two years later

"ANDI, WHAT ARE you doing?" Sean stood in the doorway of her office, his tie loosened, his hair tousled and his gray eyes worried.

"I'm making a list for my assistant. I want her to check out those crystal goblets from Ireland—"

"She's worked for you long enough to know what to do without a list," Sean argued.

"This is a special request," she said, pausing to look out the leaded panes of the window. Her desk overlooked a small, elegant garden. Now, on a late June afternoon, a soft rain was falling. Through the mist she could see the muted colors of the flowers. The garden was one of her biggest joys, and she turned away from it reluctantly, inserting her memo into the fax machine.

"You're faxing her now?"

"Of course, this will only take a minute." She tapped in the number while Sean shook his head in dismay.

"Afterward, maybe you'd like to print out a few sales graphs on the computer, or call the London

Times for an interview. And, oh, yeah, drop by Wimbledon for a set of tennis."

"My, you're being testy, luv."

"No, just nervous. And what's this 'luv' bit?"

"Merely the British equivalent of 'babe.'" Her smile was interrupted by a momentary frown. She put her hand to her forehead for an instant and then regained the smile.

"Andi," he said warningly.

"I'm fine," she reassured him as the fax went through and she put it, along with her notes, aside. "Oh, by the way, I talked to Pam a few minutes ago. Scotty got on the phone, and he said, 'I love you, Andi.'" She looked thoughtful. "Or maybe he said, 'I love candy.' Either way, he's still a genius."

"And his favorite uncle didn't get a chance to talk to him," Sean added as he hovered impatiently at the door.

"Pam was in a hurry. She had to rush Reena to the airport in Bangor. You know how your mother likes to be in the waiting room hours before the flight. Don't forget to pick her up," she reminded him. "Her flight number's on my calendar."

"And if I know Reena, she'll probably arrive ahead of schedule."

"Ahead of the *plane?*"

"Possibly. She plans ahead. Not like you," he added. "You seem determined to cut it to the last damned second—"

"I thought you'd vowed to stop swearing," she reminded him.

"You make me swear. You make me crazy. Babe, let's go, please."

She regarded him through narrowed eyes. "You're getting that look again—stressed out, tousled, anxious. What else—slightly manic?"

"My God, Andi, you're having a baby! You're in labor, and you're making lists and sending faxes. The doctor's on his way to the hospital, and where are we?"

"Getting ready to join him, if you'll give me a hand, luv."

He crossed the room and helped her out of the chair.

She leaned against him, catching her breath. "That last contraction was a doozy, I'll admit, but we still have time." She looked up at him with a mischievous grin. "Didn't you tell me when Scotty was born that you excelled in crisis situations?"

"When the crisis involves my wife and my baby, I want someone else in charge! I'm not delivering another baby, Andi, certainly not ours!"

"Okay, I'm ready. Grab my suitcase, please. Oh, and my briefcase, too."

"Your briefcase? No way."

"Just testing to see if your sense of humor is still in place."

He took her firmly by the elbow and guided her to the door. "There's only one more test I'm putting up with," he said firmly.

"And what's that?" They closed the door and walked down the pathway toward the car.

"The daddy test, babe. And I'll get four stars on that one."

"Five stars," she said, "including the one from me."

He opened the car door, attempting to get her into the passenger seat.

"Do you think we have time to stop for ice cream?"

"Get in," he ordered. "If you don't need to get to the hospital, I do."

"Okay, Daddy," she said with a grin. "Let's go."

Women throughout time have
lost their hearts to:

Starting in January 1996, Harlequin Temptation
will introduce you to five irresistible, sexy rogues.
Rogues who have carved out their place in history,
but whose true destinies lie in the arms of
contemporary women.

#569 *The Cowboy*, Kristine Rolofson
(January 1996)

#577 *The Pirate*, Kate Hoffmann
(March 1996)

#585 *The Outlaw*, JoAnn Ross
(May 1996)

#593 *The Knight*, Sandy Steen
(July 1996)

#601 *The Highwayman*, Madeline Harper
(September 1996)

Dangerous to love, impossible to resist!

Take 4 bestselling love stories FREE

Plus get a FREE surprise gift!

The Wrong Bed! The Right Man!
The Ultimate Temptation.

Beth McGruder's fantasy bed was everything she'd
imagined, except it arrived with something extra. In
her spare room, she now had a king-size monstrosity
she was dying to get rid of, and in her own room she
had the gorgeous owner, Duke McGregor, who was
anxious to take possession....

Find out what happens in
#595 LOVE ME, LOVE MY BED
by Rita Clay Estrada.

Available wherever Harlequin books are sold.

BRIDE'S BAY RESORT

UNLOCK THE DOOR TO GREAT ROMANCE AT BRIDE'S BAY RESORT

Join Harlequin's new across-the-lines series, set in an exclusive hotel on an island off the coast of South Carolina.

Seven of your favorite authors will bring you exciting stories about fascinating heroes and heroines discovering love at Bride's Bay Resort.

Look for these fabulous stories coming to a store near you beginning in January 1996.

Harlequin American Romance #613 in January
Matchmaking Baby by Cathy Gillen Thacker

Harlequin Presents #1794 in February
Indiscretions by Robyn Donald

Harlequin Intrigue #362 in March
Love and Lies by Dawn Stewardson

Harlequin Romance #3404 in April
Make Believe Engagement by Day Leclaire

Harlequin Temptation #588 in May
Stranger in the Night by Roseanne Williams

Harlequin Superromance #695 in June
Married to a Stranger by Connie Bennett

Harlequin Historicals #324 in July
Dulcie's Gift by Ruth Langan

Visit Bride's Bay Resort each month wherever Harlequin books are sold.

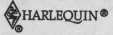

HARLEQUIN ®

BBAYG

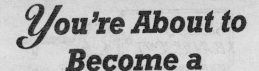

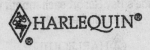